WE'RE NOT FROM HERE

GEOFF RODKEY

CROWN BOOKS
for Young Readers
New York

Text copyright © 2019 by Geoff Rodkey
Jacket art copyright © 2019 by Andrew Banneker

All rights reserved. Published in the United States by Crown Books for Young Readers, an imprint of Random House Children's Books, a division of Penguin Random House LLC, New York.

Crown and the colophon are registered trademarks of Penguin Random House LLC.

Visit us on the Web! rhcbooks.com

Educators and librarians, for a variety of teaching tools, visit us at RHTeachersLibrarians.com

Library of Congress Cataloging-in-Publication Data is available upon request.
ISBN 978-1-5247-7304-5 (trade) — ISBN 978-1-5247-7305-2 (lib. bdg.) —
ISBN 978-1-5247-7306-9 (ebook)

Printed in the United States of America
10 9 8 7 6 5 4 3 2 1
First Edition

To any kid who's ever had to start over in a new place . . .
which, in one way or another, is pretty much all of us

THE GIANT BUG RUMOR

THE FIRST TIME I heard anything about Planet Choom, we'd been on Mars for almost a year. I was sitting in the rec center with Naya and Jens. We were taking a break from shooting a video we'd written. It was either *How to Be Your Own Pet* or *Top Ten Toilets of the Mars Station*. I can't remember which.

Naya leaned in over the table and whispered, like she was telling us a big secret. "My dad says they found a planet humans can live on permanently. Like, we can breathe the air and everything. But the thing is . . ."

She looked around to make sure nobody else was listening before she went on. "There's already aliens there. And they look like giant bugs."

"What kind of bugs?" Jens asked.

"I don't know," said Naya. "I think mosquitoes."

"Are they dangerous? Like, do they have stingers?" A planet full of giant mosquitoes sounded terrifying.

Naya shook her head. "They don't *act* like mosquitoes. They just *look* like them. And they're really smart."

"As smart as humans?"

"Yeah. Like, maybe even smarter."

"Are they friendly?"

"I guess. I mean, they know we exist. And they haven't tried to kill us or anything."

"I'd rather just go to Novo," I said. This was a few months after the Governing Council had announced they'd discovered Novo in a nearby solar system. It was a planet that could almost-but-not-quite support human life, and the GC was studying whether they could "terraform" it, which meant changing its environment enough for us to live there.

Naya snorted. "Novo's never going to work," she said, shaking her head. "If it could, we'd all be headed there by now."

"Not necessarily," I told her. "Novo's really far away. So they have to be sure. And it's hard to study it from here. Plus, they need time to get all the bio-suspension pods ready." The trip to Novo would take fifteen Earth years, and the only way for a whole ship full of people to survive the trip without running out of food and water was to go into bio-suspension. Supposedly, that was just like going to sleep, except it lasted much longer, and you barfed a lot when you woke up.

"Is that what your mom told you?"

"No! It was in the weekly announcements. My mom doesn't tell me anything." Mom had been elected to the Governing Council when it got set up right after the first refugee ships arrived on Mars. It was a big deal, I guess, but it didn't get my family any special treatment or inside info. All it meant for me was that I never saw Mom, because she was always working.

"I'm just going to go back to Earth," Jens announced.

I rolled my eyes as Naya sighed. "You can't go back to Earth!" she told Jens for about the fortieth time.

"Why not?"

"Everybody there is dead!"

"So?"

"So nobody can live there anymore!"

"Nuh-uh!" Jens insisted. "We can live there again. We just have to wait a while."

"Yeah, like a thousand years."

"Nuh-uh! Just a year or two! My dad said so."

"Your dad's wrong."

"No, he's not!"

They probably would've kept arguing until Jens started to cry, which was what usually happened when we tried to change his mind about Earth. But just then an old man passed by our table. He must've been on one of the last ships to arrive, because his face was pockmarked with dark red sores from radiation exposure.

When he saw us, he stopped and looked down. "You kids making another one of your videos?"

"Yes, sir." I smiled at him, and he smiled back. Whenever we made a new video, the guy who ran Movie Night at the rec center played it on the big screen before the main feature. We'd done about half a dozen of them, and they'd turned Naya, Jens, and me into minor celebrities among the hundred or so people who usually showed up for the movie.

"Keep it up!" the man told us. "Folks need to laugh. Now more than ever."

"Not too many people laughed at the last one," Naya reminded him. I'd written *Fabulous Fashion Looks for Fall* myself, after I out-grew everything I'd brought from Earth and my parents sent me to the clothing exchange. All they had in my size were a pair of worn-out jeans with mysterious stains on them and a grimy T-shirt that said TAYLOR SWIFT WORLD TOUR 2028. Now I was stuck wearing them even though the stains grossed me out and I'd never even listened to Taylor Swift.

So I wrote a video making fun of the clothing exchange. But it came out more angry than funny, and people didn't like it nearly as much as our other ones.

"Was that the one about the clothes?" The old man grimaced in sympathy. "Yeah, that was a bit of a misfire. But don't let it get you down! You know what they say: 'Dying's easy. Comedy's hard.'"

"People say that?" I'd never heard it before. To be honest, it seemed a little inappropriate.

"They used to. Back in my theater days. Guess it made more sense back then." He chuckled. "Point is—you just keep up the good work. You're raising people's spirits. We need all the joy we can get around here." Then he put a scarred hand on my shoulder and lowered his head a little closer to mine. "Speaking of which, I heard a rumor. . . ."

I knew what was coming next even before he said it.

"Is your sister Ila Mifune? From that *Pop Singer* show?"

"Yes, sir." Ila had been playing guitar and singing since she was six. By twelve she was writing her own songs. At sixteen she went to an open audition for *Pop Singer,* the highest-rated TV show in our country. She made it all the way through to the semi-finals, where she sang one of her own songs, "Under a Blue Sky," to a TV audience of sixty million people. Going into the live final episode, she had more votes than any of the other contestants.

But the world had been slowly falling apart for a while, and two days before the episode was supposed to happen, it suddenly fell apart a lot faster. Instead of going to the airport and flying to see Ila in the *Pop Singer* finale, we wound up at the spaceport, where we were lucky enough to get seats for all four of us on a ship to Mars.

Most people weren't that lucky.

The man brightened when I told him Ila was my sister. People always did, just like they always looked crushed after they got the answers to their follow-up questions.

"You think she might grace us with that beautiful voice of hers?"

"She doesn't sing anymore, sir. I'm sorry."

"Not at all?"

"Not really, no. Says she doesn't like to perform without a guitar."

"Got to be one around here somewhere."

"No, sir. Mars has no guitars."

"She can still sing, though. Can't she?"

I nodded. "Yes, sir. But her heart's just not in it right now."

The rest of her wasn't either. Most days, my sister wouldn't even get out of bed. She'd just lie in her bunk, watching old episodes of *The Birdleys* and *Ed and Fred* on her screen. Having one of us in there 24/7 (although on Mars it was technically more like 25/7) made our shoebox-sized living compartment feel even more cramped and stuffy than it already was. Worse, Ila wasn't even nice about it. She barely looked at me except to snarl whenever I asked her to put on headphones or move her feet so I could get into our drawer.

I was pretty fed up with her moping, but Mom and Dad said I should feel sorry for her.

"When something this terrible happens," Mom told me during one of the rare times when we were alone, "it affects people in different ways. Ila hasn't been able to bounce back from it like you have. We've just got to give her time."

Personally, I thought a year (although on Mars it was technically more like half a year) should be plenty of time to bounce back. But Ila didn't seem like she was even trying. Sometimes when I came into our compartment, I'd catch the sound of one of her songs coming out of her screen. She always shut it off right away, but I suspected that when nobody else was around, she was watching her old TV performances over and over again.

It didn't seem like a healthy thing to do. Even so, when strangers like the old man asked about Ila, I smiled at them and lied a little.

"I think she'll sing again soon," I told him. "She just needs time."

"Well, you tell her she's got some big fans on this station," he said, giving my shoulder a friendly little squeeze.

"I will, sir. Thank you."

"Thank *you*. You kids have a good day now. Keep up the good work." He ambled off toward the library.

"How *is* your sister?" Naya asked me.

"Angry. Dad started making her go to the exercise room every morning."

"Angry's better than depressed, right?" Jens asked.

6

"I dunno. She's not as mean to me when she's just depressed."

"Maybe she's jealous because you're more famous than she is now," said Naya.

"That's ridiculous. Ila's *much* more famous than me."

"Not as a percentage." Naya tapped her screen open. "Think about it: Sixty million people watched that show she was on, right? But that was out of nine *billion* people on Earth." She punched the numbers into her screen's calculator. "And a hundred people watch our videos. But that's out of twenty-four hundred *total*. So according to my calculations . . ." She looked up and grinned at me. "You are six point two five times more famous on Mars than your sister was on Earth."

"That's not funny," I told Naya. "It's just sad."

Jens's shoulders slumped. "I hate math," he muttered.

I reached across the table and smacked Naya's hand. "Tell me more about these giant bug people."

"I don't know anything else," said Naya. "Just that they exist. And we asked them if we can come live on their planet."

"No way," said Jens. "It'll never happen. I mean, can you imagine? Living on a planet full of giant bugs?"

I tried to imagine it. I couldn't. It just didn't seem possible.

But then it actually happened.

2

THE INVITATION

"THEY'RE CALLED THE Zhuri," Mom told me when she got back to our living compartment late that night. "They seem very peaceful and civilized, and we're grateful they're even talking to us."

"Do they really look like giant bugs?" Ila asked. She didn't lift her head from the pillow or even look at us. But she did pause the *Birdleys* episode she was watching on her screen, which by Ila's standards meant she was incredibly interested.

"Don't call them bugs," Mom warned her. "It could be very offensive to them." Then she sighed. "But yes. They look like . . . very tall mosquitoes. And they're not the only advanced species on Planet Choom. Apparently, there are four of them, all living together in the same society. Three of the four evolved on other planets before they came to Choom. That's good for us—it means they have a history of welcoming other species as immigrants."

"Do the other species look like giant bugs too? Or just the Zhuri?"

Mom gave me an annoyed frown. "Lan, seriously—don't call them bugs."

"Sorry," I said. "But do they?"

Mom shrugged. "We don't know yet. There's a lot we don't know. It's been hard to communicate. The lag time between here and Choom is huge, and we're still trying to get a handle on their language. By the way—whatever you do, don't discuss this with anybody until the GC makes an official announcement tomorrow."

Mom looked at me as she said that. Since Ila never left our compartment unless my parents insisted, the odds of my sister discussing anything with anybody were pretty slim.

"Can we talk to Dad about it?"

"Yes. But you probably won't see him. He's working late again tonight." Back on Earth, Dad had been a scientist. On Mars, he was part of a group in the Nutrition Department that was trying to create a food substitute. It was important work, because everybody knew that sooner or later we'd run out of the rations we'd brought from Earth. As far as I could tell from a couple of whispered conversations I'd overheard between Mom and Dad, that was happening faster than a lot of people thought. Dad and the rest of his group had been working around the clock for weeks.

"What's the GC going to tell people?" Ila asked Mom.

"Just that Planet Choom and the Zhuri exist, and that the Governing Council's talking to them about accepting human refugees. But it might not happen. And if it does, it'll take a while."

• • •

IT TOOK LONGER than a while. In the end, it was another eight months before the Zhuri officially invited humans to Choom. By then, life on the Mars station was grim. The air processors were wearing down, which made the oxygen levels drop so much that everybody felt tired all the time. Water rationing got so strict that people could only shower every ten days, so the whole station smelled like an armpit.

People's clothes were turning not just stinky, but ragged. Even on limited rations, I'd somehow managed to keep growing until I had to go back to the exchange and swap my stained jeans and Taylor Swift tee for a scratchy YOMIURI GIANTS jersey and a pair of beat-up khakis with holes in both knees, which kept reopening no matter how many times I sewed them back together.

The biggest problem, though, was the food. When the Earth supplies ran out, Dad's team in Nutrition introduced Chow, and everybody hated it. It came in three flavors: Curry, Berry, and Harvest. Within a few days, people had started calling them Choking, Barfing, and Heaving.

After a month of nothing but Chow to eat, the food protests started. Dad took it personally. When people stopped him in the hallways to complain, he'd give them a tight smile and say things like, "We're doing the best we can with the resources we've got," and "I know it leaves a lot to be desired, but Chow's keeping us alive."

Back in our compartment at night, he was a lot less polite. "It's ridiculous!" he'd vent to Mom. "What did they expect? Lobster Newburg?"

When Naya, Jens, and I made *Top Ten Recipes for Chow,* and one of them was Lobster Newburg, Dad didn't think it was funny. A lot of other people did, though. Judging by the laughter when it first played, it was one of our most popular videos.

But we stopped screening it after the food riot happened. The riot was terrifying. Eleven people were injured, and during the worst of it, we had to barricade ourselves inside our compartment while rioters pounded on our door and yelled for Mom and Dad to come out. Security got things under control eventually, but it was a couple of weeks before Mom let me walk around the station by myself again. Even after that, every time I left our compartment, a little knot of fear settled into the pit of my stomach, and it didn't go away for the rest of our time on Mars.

The situation might've gotten even worse after the riot, but then the problems with the air processors started, and the lack of oxygen made everybody too tired to cause trouble.

"They did it on purpose," Jens told Naya and me. "My dad says the GC lowered the oxygen levels just to control people."

I was pretty sure that wasn't true, but I was too tired and hungry to argue with him.

All of us were tired and hungry (not to mention smelly and desperate) by the time the GC crammed us all into the cafeteria to watch the government of Planet Choom's official offer of refuge to the entire human race. They moved the big screen over from the rec center for the occasion, and Mom stood under it with Dr. Chang and General Schiller to introduce the video.

Mom started by telling us all how kind and selfless the people of Choom were, what a precious gift the invitation was, and what a great job the Diplomacy Department had done negotiating with Choom's government.

Then Dr. Chang asked us to turn on the translator apps the GC had pushed to our screens the night before.

"You should be able to hear a clean translation of the Zhuri through your earpieces," she said. "Unfortunately, while we've been told that everyone in the video is speaking the Zhuri language, our translation program can't comprehend the accents of the Krik, Ororo, and Nug people. We've prepared subtitles for those sections, so please keep an eye on the video screen. And now . . . here's the invitation."

Mom and the other two leaders stepped aside, the screen came to life, and four very different-looking aliens appeared on it, in a wide shot that let us view them from head to foot.

Except that not all of them had feet.

At the first sight of the aliens, there were gasps from the crowd. A couple of people shrieked in fear. "Mercy!" cried a woman from somewhere behind me.

I didn't gasp or yell, but my whole body went weak, and my heart started to thump.

They just looked so . . . *alien.*

Taking up the whole left side of the screen was an Ororo: a giant, white-blue marshmallow with sleepy dark eyes. It must've had legs, but its body was so thick and blobby I couldn't see them. As it lumbered toward the camera with the others, its flesh quivered like an enormous bowl of gelatin.

In the middle of the screen, leading the group toward the camera, was a Zhuri. I'd seen plenty of photos of them by this point, so the sticklike body, huge compound eyes, tube-shaped mouth, and long wings that folded down its back weren't a surprise. But the bendy-legged, funny-scary way it walked was deeply weird. Watching it move, I didn't know whether to laugh or scream.

On the near right, and less than half as tall as the others, was a Krik: a fuzzy little green werewolf with bulging muscles, red eyes, and an enormous mouth with double rows of razor-sharp gray teeth. If it hadn't been so short, it would've looked terrifying, although I wondered later if it only seemed short because the others were so tall.

Finally, there was a Nug. It was the strangest of the four—a massive wormlike creature that slithered forward in an L shape, its slick body topped by a gaping hole. It was like a combination of an eggplant, a sea slug, and an open garbage can.

The four of them moved to what I guessed was a few feet in front of the camera, then stopped. The Zhuri's tube-shaped mouth vibrated as it began to speak in a high-pitched whine:

"Yeeeeeeeyeeeeeeeh . . ."

A moment later, the translation came through my earpiece. The translator app had given the Zhuri a voice signature that sounded like a gentle elderly man. In a weird way, the voice was almost soothing—it was much less scary listening to a giant mosquito talk when it sounded like somebody's kindly old grandpa:

"On behalf of the Unified Government of Choom, we send greetings to the humans and offer our sorrow at the loss of your home planet. All four of our species, at earlier stages in our development, suffered from varying degrees of self-inflicted violence. But just as we evolved beyond violence, we are confident the human species can do so too.

"Thus we offer you refuge among us, that you may live and

13

thrive in our multispecies society. As long as you remain peaceful, you are welcome here."

The Zhuri's body bobbed up and down as it stepped back on its bendy stick legs. Then the muscular little Krik came forward and opened its toothy mouth.

"GZZZRRRRGZZRRRKKKKKK..."

Its voice was a rough, snappish growl. The translator app beeped in my ear. "Unknown language detected," it said as the Krik's message appeared in a subtitle on the big screen:

> **The Krik have always lived on Planet Choom. We
> like it here.**
> **You may join us if you do not make it worse.**

The Krik stepped back, and the giant-marshmallow Ororo glooped forward.

"MRRRRUMMMMRRRRMMM..."

The Ororo's voice was so deep that, even through the speakers, I could practically feel the vibrations in my chest as the translator beeped helplessly in my ear again.

> **The Ororo are not bothered by the thought of
> your arrival.**

It seemed like a strange thing to say. But I didn't have time to dwell on it, because the Nug was already slithering forward with its own greeting.

"SKRRRREEEEREEEREEEREE...!"

The Nug's voice was so loud and screechy that it drowned

out my translator's "unknown language" message. People around me covered their ears, and even the other three aliens in the video seemed to lean away from the Nug and grimace uncomfortably as it shrieked its welcome.

> **Hello! The Nug are Planet Choom's newest immigrants!**
> **We are excited to meet you!**
> **We hope you will share in our celebrations!**
> **HEE-HAW!**

The Nug's final *"SKREEE-SKREEE!"* was so loud that I felt like I'd been stabbed in the ears with a pair of forks. Fortunately, it stopped talking and slithered backward after that.

The Zhuri leader loped forward again on its springy legs. "We hope you will accept our invitation. Your journey to Choom will be long, but a new home awaits you here, and we are eager to meet you. Until then, may your travels be safe."

The video ended. There was an uneasy silence as General Schiller walked back to the front of the room to address us. Mom and Dr. Chang trailed behind him.

"I think it goes without saying," the general told us, "that this is a real unusual situation. It'll take some getting used to. But all of us on the GC are in strong agreement that if we want the human race to continue, Planet Choom's our best bet. We hope you feel the same."

As it turned out, though, not everybody wanted to move in with the strange-looking aliens and their earsplitting screeches.

Some people wanted to hold out for terraforming Novo, even

though the GC warned that they still didn't have enough data to know if it was possible. Dr. Chang suggested that the Novo group come to Choom first. It was twice as close to Novo as Mars, so it'd be much easier to study Novo and launch a trip from there. But the Novo faction didn't want anything to do with Choom. In the end, four hundred of them decided to stay on Mars and prepare to go straight to Novo.

Even more shocking were the almost nine hundred people who voted to go back to Earth. All the scientists agreed it wouldn't be livable again for hundreds of years, but the Earthers refused to believe them.

Jens and his dad were Earthers. "You'll see," Jens told Naya and me. "It's going to be fine. Once you're off living with those alien freaks, you're going to wish you were back on Earth with us."

I was sure he was wrong, but I didn't argue with him. It wouldn't have helped unless I could've somehow changed Jens's dad's mind too. And Mom and Dad both told me that was impossible.

"People believe what they want to believe," Dad said with a shrug.

In the end, all Naya and I could do was hug Jens and tell him we'd keep in touch.

"That'll be super weird," he said. "You're going to spend the next twenty years in bio-suspension. By the time you get out of it, I'll be, like, your dad's age."

"I sure hope so," Naya said.

"What do you mean?"

"Nothing." Then she hugged him again.

I hugged him too. "Be safe, okay?"

"You too. Send videos."

"We will."

Then Naya and I joined Ila, my parents, and 1,018 other people on the shuttle up to the transport that waited in low orbit to take us to Planet Choom. The living conditions on the transport were even worse than the Mars station—nobody had their own compartment, and we all had to sleep in our bio-suspension pods, which were in one giant room together.

Fortunately, we were only on the transport for two days before we all went into suspension and woke up the next morning—or twenty years later, depending on how you looked at it—in a solar system sixty trillion miles away, ready to start a new life on Choom.

But there was a problem. During the twenty years we were asleep, the aliens had changed their minds about us.

3

NEVER MIND, CAN YOU JUST GO AWAY?

THE FIRST THING I heard when I came out of suspension was Mom's voice.

"Hey, Lan," she was saying. "Hey. Hey. Time to get up, Lan."

I could feel her fingertips gently pushing the hair off my forehead. When I opened my eyes, she was smiling down at me. I smiled back and sat up.

Then I barfed.

Or I would've, if there'd been anything in my stomach. Since it was empty (they don't let you go to sleep for twenty years on a full stomach), I mostly just dry-heaved into the little bucket Mom held for me.

"It's okay," she said as she patted my back. "Everybody does that when they come out of it."

"Why aren't you doing it?"

"I've been up for a day or so. Your father has too."

"Morning, sunshine." I looked up and saw Dad sitting on the edge of Ila's pod, holding her hair back while her face was buried in her own bucket. "Long time no see."

"It doesn't feel like it," I said, looking across the crowded pod room. Everyone was like us—either just getting up, or holding a bucket for someone who was just getting up.

"It's weird, right? Twenty years went by, just like that."

I heaved again. "How close are we to Choom?"

"Pretty close," said Mom. "We're in orbit."

"Are we landing soon?"

Mom and Dad looked at each other. "Well . . ."

What?" Mom's tone of voice sent Ila's head jerking up out of her bucket. My sister's face was gray, and there were fat, dark circles under her eyes. She narrowed them at Mom. "What's going on?"

"There's been a complication," Mom said in a quiet voice. "As soon as everybody's awake, we'll explain it."

AN HOUR LATER, Mom stood at the front of the pod room with Dr. Chang and General Schiller, just like they had when they'd played the invitation video for us back on Mars.

This time around, they didn't look excited. They looked worried.

"When the first of us came out of bio-suspension," General Schiller explained, "we radioed Choom's government for landing instructions. Instead of answering, they sent this video. We figured you'd best see it for yourselves."

The communal screens on each wall of the room flickered to life with the image of a single Zhuri in close-up, its compound eyes fixed on the camera.

"*Heeeeyeeeeeeeheee . . .*"

After a moment, the translator kicked in:

"The Unified Government of Choom regrets to inform you that our people have agreed the human species is too violent and emotional to live among us. Our society has no conflict. Your presence would threaten our peace.

"For your safety and ours, we ask that you leave our orbit immediately. Please do not attempt to enter Choom's atmosphere, or our defensive weapons will vaporize you. We wish you safe travels and a pleasant future. Goodbye."

Then the video ended, and the yelling began.

There was a lot of crying too.

The yelling and crying went on for a long time, mostly because there was nothing else we could do. The GC had sent a dozen messages down to Planet Choom since getting the video, but nobody would answer them.

It didn't seem like the GC's fault to me. A lot of people blamed them anyway.

"How can you let them *do* this? They *invited* us here!"

"It's as big a mystery to us as it is to you," Dr. Chang said.

"Did you lie to them or something? Are they just finding out now what humans are really like?"

"Absolutely not," said Mom. "We were open with them from the beginning about Earth's entire history. We sent thousands of hours of historical and cultural videos. They knew everything there was to know about us."

"We gave them the whole kit and caboodle," General Schiller agreed. "Warts and all. That's why it took them so long to invite us in the first place."

Most people wanted to leave Choom's orbit right away. But

we couldn't, because we didn't have enough fuel left to go anywhere.

Even if we did, there was no place to go.

"We haven't logged a message from the Novo group since six months after we left Mars," Dr. Chang explained. "At that point, they'd just begun their journey. We've heard nothing further since they entered bio-suspension."

"Are they okay?" someone asked.

"We don't know," said Dr. Chang. "They'd been having problems with their communications array. The radio silence could be that . . . or something worse."

"Why don't we go to Novo?" someone else suggested.

Dr. Chang shook her head. "We're close enough now to analyze Novo's atmosphere. It has no oxygen. Terraforming it is beyond our ability. We can't live there."

"What about the Earthers? How are they doing?"

This time, all three of the GC members shook their heads sadly. "They went dark pretty soon after they got to Earth," said General Schiller. "The final message made it clear things didn't work out too well for them."

My eyes welled up as I thought about Jens and the others.

"Let's just go back to Mars!" somebody called out.

There was more head shaking from the GC. "Even if we had the fuel," Mom explained, "by the time we got there, the station would've spent forty years exposed to Martian windstorms. Its life-support systems would've failed a long time ago."

"This is nonsense!" bellowed a tall, red-faced man named Gunderson. He'd been a football coach back on Earth, and he still seemed to get a kick out of yelling like one. "Are you telling me we spent twenty years burning fuel, crossing half a galaxy, just to turn around again 'cause these folks got cold feet? I say we call their bluff! Put ourselves down on that planet and tell them we ain't taking no for an answer!"

Some people really liked hearing that. They clapped and whistled. But General Schiller wasn't impressed. "Mr. Gunderson," he said in a low but firm voice, "Choom's society is fundamentally peaceful—but that warning in the video about vaporizing us was no joke. These folks have weapons technology that makes us look like cavemen throwing rocks. We call their bluff, we're going to get our heads handed to us.

"More than that," the general added, "I want to remind you that the kind of thinking that says we can get what we want by attacking people was what cost us our planet in the first place. I'd like to believe we all learned a lesson from that. I know I did."

Gunderson didn't like getting scolded by a general. He crossed his arms and stuck out his jaw like a pouty little kid. "What the heck else are we gonna do?"

"We're going to keep trying to talk to these people," replied Schiller, "and pray they start talking back."

After that, Mom delivered a big pep talk about how it was a scary situation, but we were going to get through it together, and in the end we'd all look back and be proud of how we'd helped save the human race and met this challenge with courage, and unity, and good cheer. I think it must've been really inspiring, but I didn't hear a word of it, because I was so anxious and scared that I couldn't think straight, let alone listen to a speech. I didn't sleep a wink that night, and it wasn't just because I'd gotten twenty years' worth of sleep the night before.

Considering all the sniffles, whimpers, and muffled tears echoing through the darkened pod room that night, I don't think anybody else slept either.

AFTER WE'D SPENT a couple of very bad days in orbit, Choom's government finally started to talk to us. At first they just traded messages with the GC—mostly apologies, along with more requests for us to leave. But then Mom managed to talk them into doing a live videoconference in the pod room with the whole group of us.

"But we look *awful*," Ila said when she heard the news, and it was true. What was left of the human race looked exactly like you'd expect from a room full of starving people who hadn't changed their clothes in twenty years.

Mom just nodded. "That's the whole point. If they can see us, they might feel some sympathy. And they'll realize we're not a threat to them."

So when the videoconference began and the lone Zhuri's insect-like head appeared on the communal screens, we all did our best to look pitiful, helpless, and friendly all at once. It was a tough combination to pull off.

"Greetings," said the Zhuri. Our translator apps gave her the voice signature of a squeaky-sounding little girl, which would've been funny if the situation weren't so serious. "My name is Leeni. I am a senior official in the Immigration Division of the Unified Government of Choom. On behalf of our people, I apologize that you are no longer welcome."

Mom had been given the job of speaking for all of us.

23

"Greetings to you, Leeni," she said as her translator turned her words into the *yeeeehheee* whine that the Zhuri could understand. "My name is Amora Persaud. I am a member of the Governing Council of the human race. We humbly ask that you reconsider your decision."

Mom waved her hand to indicate the thousand of us who stood behind her. "As you can see," she explained, "we are a weak, helpless, and desperate group. If you admit us to Choom, we promise to cause no violence and do no harm. If we break this promise, we will leave immediately. We wish only to live in peace, with your mercy and help."

The Zhuri took so long to answer that I started to wonder if the data connection was broken. Finally she spoke again.

"Everyone here agrees," she said, "that it is best if the human does not come to Choom."

"With all respect," Mom replied, "we are only here because you invited us. And we have nowhere else to go."

"That invitation was a long time ago," the Zhuri said. "Since then, there have been many changes in the Unified Government. Those who invited you are no longer our leaders. Now everyone agrees that for your own safety as well as ours, you should not come here."

"We have nowhere else to go," Mom repeated in a firm voice. "There is very little food and even less fuel on this ship. We used nearly all we had in order to come to you—as you requested. If you do not let us land, *we will die.*"

There were gasps and whimpers all around me. I knew the situation was bad, but hearing Mom say that out loud made my whole body turn weak with fear.

Mom's voice somehow stayed calm. "You say you love peace," she told the Zhuri. "If so, how can you allow this to happen?"

It was impossible to tell what the Zhuri was thinking. Her compound eyes and her tube-shaped mouth never moved. But the pause before she answered was even longer than before.

"We will call you back," she finally said.

Then the screen went dark.

THE NEXT DAY, Naya and I were sitting on my pod, playing Monopoly on her screen. Ila was next to us, lying on her own pod and watching TV, when Mom and Dad practically sprinted across the room to us. They'd been in the control room, and it was obvious from their faces that something big had just happened.

"What is it?" I asked.

"Choom's government agreed to open the planet to one 'human reproductive unit,'" Mom told us, grinning from ear to ear as she made air quotes around "human reproductive unit."

"They're letting in one family as a test case," Dad explained. "If it works out, we think they'll let in everybody else."

My sister's eyes widened. "The family's not going to be us, is it?"

It was us.

WELCOME TO CHOOM

"MY BUTT DOESN'T fit in this seat," Ila complained.

The government of Choom had sent an empty shuttle on autopilot to take the four of us down to the planet. It had thirty-two bucket seats in eight rows, all made for rail-skinny Zhuri and half as wide as normal human seats. Somehow we had to figure out how to sit in them to strap ourselves down for the entry into Choom's atmosphere.

"Nobody's butt fits, honey," Dad told Ila. "Let's just make the best of it."

I tried to straddle the dividing ridge between two seats, but it was too high and sharp. Then I tried to sit cockeyed, with half of my butt riding up on one side of the seat, but that made my back hurt. And balancing myself across two of the dividers hurt even more.

The rest of my family was having the same problem. Dad finally solved it by having us fill the seat buckets with our extra clothing to raise them up to the level of the dividers.

An extra set of clothing was my biggest **perk** as a member of the First Human Family to Go to Choom. I don't know how many owners the light blue cotton shirt and navy pants with rolled-up cuffs had been through before me, but I was grateful none of them had spilled anything nasty enough to leave a stain.

After I filled my bucket seat with a folded pile of my ragged khakis and grimy Giants jersey, I managed to strap myself in. Once I clicked the harness fastener, some kind of auto-tightener kicked in, squeezing me against the seat so hard I could barely breathe.

"This thing's *strangling* me," Ila whined from the row behind me. "How long is this trip going to take?"

"I don't know, Ila. I've never made it before," Mom replied, almost but not quite keeping the irritation out of her voice.

Ila's attitude had gone through some major swings since we'd found out we'd been picked to go to Choom. At first she didn't want to go at all. Then Mom explained that Ila was a big part of why the GC had chosen our family.

"We need your voice," Mom told her. "When we were nego-tiating with them before we left Mars, the Zhuri seemed very ex-cited about our art forms. Especially music. Having a human down there who can perform live could be huge in winning them over."

"But I don't have a guitar!"

"We figured you could sing a cappella," Dad said.

"Ugh!" Ila screwed up her face. "How many times have I told you I can't—"

"*Ila.* Think about the situation we're in."

Mom didn't come right out and say *The fate of the human race could depend on your singing.* She didn't have to. Ila was difficult, but she wasn't stupid.

27

"I guess I could sing 'Home, Sweet Home,'" she said after she'd thought about it for a while.

"That's perfect!" Mom and Dad looked at each other. "And maybe," Mom said in a gentle voice, "you could rehearse a little up here before we leave—"

"No." Ila shook her head. "I don't need to rehearse."

"Ila," Dad told her, "you *have* to rehearse."

She never did, and I could tell it made my parents nervous. The plan was for Ila to sing "Home, Sweet Home" right after Mom gave a welcome speech when we landed on Choom, and even though my sister swore her voice would be fine, nobody could really be sure without having heard her sing in twenty years. But Mom and Dad didn't push her. I think they were just glad to see her quit watching TV and get out of bed. In the day and a half before we left for Choom, Ila seemed more energetic and talkative than she had been since Earth. She even managed to make small talk with people, which she hadn't done in forever.

At one point, I saw a chatty friend of Mom's put an excited hand on Ila's arm and crow, "They're just going to *love* you down there! Once they hear that voice of yours? You'll be a bigger star than you were on Earth!"

My sister's eyes lit up like fireworks at the idea. "I don't know about *that*," Ila replied, but the way she said it sounded more like *Ohmygosh that would be amazing and now I have a reason for living again!*

It seemed like Ila wasn't half as excited about helping save the human race as she was about being the center of everybody's attention. I knew that sounded horrible, so I kept it to myself.

But she did make me wish I had something useful to contribute instead of just being along for the ride.

"So if Mom's going to give a speech, and Ila's going to sing, what are our jobs?" I asked Dad.

"We just have to smile a lot," he told me. "Our jobs are to be the happiest, friendliest, most fun-to-be-around species of all time."

"So, basically, we should act like human golden retrievers?"

Dad grinned. "*Exactly* like that."

I thought it was funny enough to tell Naya, but she didn't react like I thought she would.

"It just makes me think about how there aren't any more golden retrievers," she said.

"Oh geez. I'm sorry."

We dropped the subject, but when the empty shuttle from Choom showed up and it was time to say goodbye, she hugged me and said, "Be a really good doggie for the aliens, okay?"

"I will. Ruff, ruff."

"Seriously. I *really* want to get off this ship."

"I know. I'll be awesome. I'll be so amazing, they'll all want to adopt me and give me treats. And maybe put a bandanna around my neck."

She hugged me again. "Good luck. Ruff, ruff."

Then I got on the shuttle in a hurry, because I was scared out of my mind, and I didn't want Naya to notice. The four of us fixed the too-skinny seat problem, then watched as the last human from maintenance left the shuttle and sealed the air lock behind him with a hiss.

"How's everybody feeling?" Dad asked from his seat next to Ila in the row behind me and Mom.

"Terrified," I said. We hadn't even started moving, and my stomach already felt like it was permanently stuck on the first big drop of a giant roller coaster.

Mom reached out and took my hand. "It's okay to be scared. We can be scared and brave at the same time."

"Why don't we all pray?" Dad suggested, and we did.

It helped a little.

A moment later, the shuttle detached, and we watched the transport disappear from the right-hand windows. I was strapped in too tight to move, but once we were free of the transport's manufactured gravity, I could feel my hair start to float up.

"We're going to do great," Mom said. "We're going to be our best selves, and they're all going to realize how awesome humans are."

Nobody said anything for a minute after that. Then I heard Dad ask Ila:

"Do you want to rehearse your song?"

"No."

"You sure? Just once?"

"No! It'll be fine."

WE DIDN'T SPEND long in zero gravity. Ten minutes later, we were roaring down through the upper atmosphere, the whole ship shuddering like it might fly apart. The g-forces were so bad that I thought my chest was going to crumple like a soda can.

Then the g-forces weakened, the ride smoothed out, and a cloudy sky appeared through the small side windows.

"It's green," Ila said. "The sky is *green*."

"It sure is," Dad agreed.

"But we can breathe the air, right?"

"It's twenty-five percent oxygen. Not only can we breathe it—we're going to feel fantastic. Although the gravity will be a little heavier than we're used to."

"Can I unstrap my harness and look out the window?" I asked.

"Wait until we land," Mom told me. "It's too dangerous now."

I stayed put and tried to crane my neck to get a better look out the side windows. We kept descending, and pretty soon we were low enough to see the ground. It was a single color of beige all the way to the horizon, rumpled with hundreds of perfectly shaped, six-sided hills of varying heights.

It took a moment for me to realize those weren't hills. It was an endless city of buildings all made in the exact same shape, with just a few scattered hexes of red to break up the dreary beige color. It was like looking at a planet-sized beehive.

"You know what they could use?" Dad asked. "Architecture."

"That's good for us," said Mom. "We can give them architecture."

We came to a brief stop in midair, about fifty yards up. I could hear a whine like a busted air conditioner from somewhere below us. Then the shuttle began to descend.

Halfway to the ground, there was a sudden *BZZZZZT!* as loud as a thunderclap. Blue light flashed through the windows as all the hairs on my body stood on end.

It felt like we'd been hit by lightning. "What was *that*?" Ila yelled.

Before anybody could answer, the ship touched down. The blue light kept flashing outside, accompanied by the same crackling *BZZZZT!,* and the broken-air-conditioner whine was much louder.

I looked out the left-hand window. We were on the tarmac of some kind of spaceport. A hundred yards away, where the tarmac met the first row of low beige buildings, there was a massive greenish-brown cloud rising from the ground about twenty yards high.

The air-conditioner noise was coming from the giant cloud. The crackling buzz erupted again, and the cloud shimmered as a giant sheet of blue electricity appeared for an instant right in front of it.

Ila ran to one of the left-side windows, peering out as the sheet of blue electricity lit up again.

"Ohmygosh!" she yelled. "Those are *aliens!*"

I got out of my harness and joined her at the windows. She was right. The cloud was a living swarm of thousands of giant-mosquito Zhuri, flitting in midair and whining in their *yeeeeeeheee* language.

Dad looked out the window beside Ila. "They're not aliens," he said. "They live here. From now on, *we're* the aliens."

I stared at the swarm of Zhuri on the other side of the crackling, on-and-off sheet of electricity. They were buzzing back and forth, jostling each other in a frenzy. When the sheet of electricity lit up again, I saw one of them shoot backward like they'd been electrocuted.

"Must be an electric fence," Dad said. "See how it lights up when they touch it?"

"What are they yelling?" Ila asked.

We were turning on our translators when Mom called to us from the other side of the ship.

"Come over here! There's a welcoming party."

We went over to the right side of the ship and looked out. About thirty yards from us, there was a stage set up on the tarmac. Standing on it were three stick-skinny Zhuri, a giant-marshmallow Ororo, and a little-green-werewolf Krik. They looked like they were waiting to begin our welcoming ceremony.

A cluster of about twenty more Zhuri and a few Krik were in front of the stage, all of them turned to face us.

On either side of the small audience, standing in two lines that ran from the stage all the way to our shuttle, were a couple dozen Zhuri holding yard-long metal sticks with two prongs on one end.

The way they held those pronged sticks reminded me of soldiers carrying weapons. But I knew the Zhuri were peaceful, so I figured they couldn't actually be weapons.

My translator was on, but the swarm of Zhuri behind us was too far away for the app to pick up whatever they were yelling. A moment later, though, the shuttle's speakers came to life with a *"YEEHEEEEE . . ."* that the translator quickly converted:

"PLEASE EXIT THE SHIP."

The frame of the cabin door lit up in a glowing invitation. As we walked toward it, I tried to take a couple of deep breaths to calm myself down.

"Are we ready?" Dad asked.

33

"Just remember," Mom told us, "we're the kindest, friendliest, most peaceful species in the history of the universe."

The handle on the door was blinking. Dad twisted it to open the air lock, and we took our first steps onto Planet Choom.

It was warm and humid, with a heavy smell of gasoline in the air. As I looked up at the green sky, I heard the electric crackle again, and when the blue light flashed, I realized it wasn't just a straight fence—it formed a giant dome that covered the whole tarmac, thirty yards high and a couple hundred yards across.

The electric dome vanished for half a second, then lit up again with another *BZZZZZZT!*

The double rows of Zhuri holding their metal prongs were just a few feet away on either side, staring at us with their blank compound eyes. As the four of us started to walk toward the stage, each Zhuri shifted their metal prong in their hands, pointing at us as we passed.

If they weren't soldiers training weapons on us, they were doing a *really* good imitation of soldiers training weapons on us.

I hoped nobody could tell I was practically shaking with fear.

The swarm was behind us, a hundred yards away on the other side of the dome. Now that we were outside, the yells were distinct enough that my translator started to pick up a few stray words:

"HUMANS . . ."

"HOME . . ."

"PLANET . . ."

"HUMANS . . ."

Up ahead, one of the Zhuri on the stage took a bendy-legged step forward and spoke into a small, hovering sphere that must've

34

been a microphone, because his voice boomed out across the tarmac. *"EEEEEYEEEEHEEE . . ."*

"THE UNIFIED GOVERNMENT OF CHOOM WELCOMES THE HUMAN TO OUR PLANET—"

That was as far as he got, because as soon as he started to talk, the swarm's yells turned into screams, there was a *BZZZZT!* that didn't stop, and the dome lit up—only this time, it stayed lit.

For a long, frightening second, the blue light shining on us from every direction nearly blinded me as the *BZZZZZT!* drowned out everything else.

Then the dome vanished, and the noise stopped. The whole electrical field had shut down.

There was a split second of quiet. Everyone who was facing us—all the Zhuri, the handful of Krik, and the lone Ororo—looked up, then drew their heads back in surprise.

The two dozen soldier-like Zhuri with the long metal prongs all took to the air, flying past us over our heads.

As they did, the whole crowd in front of us turned and ran—or flew—away. I was staring at them in shock, wondering how the big blobby-looking Ororo could run so fast, when Mom grabbed my arm.

"GET BACK IN THE SHIP!" she screamed.

I turned in the direction she was pulling me.

That's when I realized the swarm was coming for us. The whole seething cloud of thousands of Zhuri was halfway across the tarmac, shrieking as they zoomed through the air straight at me.

I stumbled as I ran for the shuttle and almost didn't get back in time. Half a second after Dad slammed the door shut behind me, the first wave of attackers hit the ship.

5

BUT SERIOUSLY,
PLEASE GO AWAY

THE ZHURI WERE spitting some kind of liquid on our shuttle. We could hear it splatter against the roof and sides. It was running down the windows in such thick orange smears that pretty soon we couldn't see outside. A heavy gasoline stink filled the inside of the shuttle. Breathing it in made me want to retch.

The screams of the Zhuri were so loud that the translator had no trouble picking up the words now.

"GO HOME!"

"DIE HUMANS!"

"ALIEN SCUM!"

"LEAVE OUR PLANET!"

I took out my earpiece so I wouldn't have to hear the words. Dad hugged me tight. Mom was trying to comfort Ila, who was freaking out.

We'd been through some scary moments during our last hours on Earth. In some ways the food riot on Mars had been even scarier. But this was much, much worse than either of those.

"It's going to be okay," Mom kept saying.

"We're safe in here," Dad said as he rubbed my back. "Don't worry."

Worry didn't even come close to describing it. I was petrified.

It's hard to say how long the attack went on. It felt like forever, but it could've been as little as half a minute before we heard an amplified Zhuri voice outside on the tarmac, broadcasting over the screams of the swarm. I put my earpiece back in to hear what it was telling the attackers:

"YOU ARE DISPLAYING EXCESSIVE SMELL. CLEAR THE AIR AND EXIT THE LANDING AREA IMMEDIATELY."

The announcement kept repeating, over and over again. Slowly the *splat-splat-splat* of the spitting attacks slacked off, and the angry screams quieted a bit. We started to hear a new noise—a crackling *BZZZT!* like the sound the dome had made, only lower-pitched and not as loud.

Then the attacks stopped completely, and enough orange muck slid off the windows that we were able to get a blurry look outside.

The Zhuri soldiers were using their long metal prongs to force the swarm away from our shuttle. The prongs seemed to work like cattle prods—when they touched one of the attackers, there was a *BZZZT!* and a little blue arc of electricity, and the attacker would get zapped back about half a foot before dropping onto the tarmac.

Then it would lie there twitching for a few seconds before it staggered to its feet and flew away in a dizzy, confused-looking path.

It took maybe ten minutes for the Zhuri soldiers to clear

everyone away from the shuttle. By then the gasoline stink was fading, and Ila had calmed down enough to talk.

"I thought they were peaceful!"

Mom stroked Ila's hair. "So did I, sweetheart."

"What are we going to do?" I asked.

"We're going to wait," Mom said.

A few seconds later, a Zhuri voice came through our shuttle's speakers with instructions for us:

"DO NOT EXIT THE SHIP. REMAIN IN PLACE."

They didn't need to worry. We weren't going anywhere. A minute later, there was another announcement from the shuttle speakers:

"THE UNIFIED GOVERNMENT OF CHOOM APOLOGIZES FOR THIS DISTURBANCE. WE ARE CLEARING THE AIR OF EMOTION. DO NOT EXIT THE SHIP."

Eventually they managed to clear all the attackers off the tarmac and get the electric fencing up again. Then some kind of hover truck came out, and a bunch of little green Krik wearing these weird pants-free overalls—which were the first clothes I'd seen on any of Choom's creatures—hosed down the ship, cleaning all the orange muck off of it. After that, we watched another group of Krik workers take down the stage that had been set up for our arrival.

"So much for the welcoming ceremony," Dad said as they carted off the pieces.

"We can't stay here," said Ila. "We have to get off this planet."

"Let's just take things one step at a time," Mom told her. "We're safe right now. That's the important thing."

After the Krik workers finished cleaning the shuttle, they flew off in the hover truck, leaving the tarmac empty. Then nothing happened for a long time, except that the speakers occasionally reminded us not to go anywhere:

"DO NOT EXIT THE SHIP. AWAIT FURTHER INSTRUCTIONS."

We sat there for a couple of hours. Over time it got less scary and more boring. Eventually Ila and I started watching *Birdleys* episodes. We were on our third one when the shuttle began to move.

It taxied across the tarmac and into an open hangar, which closed behind us. The shuttle came to a stop.

"PLEASE EXIT THE SHIP."

The frame of the exit door lit up again, its handle blinking for us to open it. We all went to the right-hand windows and looked out.

Half a dozen Zhuri soldiers stood on either side of the exit door, holding pronged weapons. Between them, two unarmed Zhuri waited, facing the door.

"What if they attack us?" Ila asked.

"They're not going to attack," Mom said. "I promise." The rest of us followed her to the exit.

"Remember," Dad told us as he put his hand on the door handle, "we're friendly and peaceful."

"They just tried to kill us!" Ila yelped.

"I didn't say it'd be easy."

Dad twisted the door open, and we put our feet down on Planet Choom for the second time. Now that I knew they could deliver a jolt of paralyzing electricity, the pronged weapons pointing at us from both sides were even scarier. I tried to smile as I walked behind Mom and Dad toward the two unarmed Zhuri.

But the guards shifted their weapons to follow us with each step, and it's tough to smile when you're afraid you could get electrocuted at any second.

"Greetings," said one of the Zhuri. The translator gave him a gruff, raspy voice. "I am Heeor. I represent the Executive Division of the Unified Government of Choom."

A funky sour-milk stink was filling my nose, making it even harder to smile.

"I am Leeni of the Immigration Division," the second one said. She must've been the same official who'd spoken to us in the videoconference, because the translator app—which had thousands of human voice signatures in its library, and was programmed to assign a specific one to each Zhuri so we could tell them apart by their voices—gave her the same squeaky little-girl signature as before.

"Greetings," Mom said to them. "I am Amora Persaud of the Governing Council of the human species. This is my husband, Kalil Mifune, and our children, Ila and Lan."

The sour-milk smell was getting worse. It seemed to be coming from the Zhuri themselves.

"We apologize for the disturbance following your arrival," the gruff-sounding one said. "There was a mechanical failure in the protective fencing."

"May I ask what exactly happened?" said Mom in her most diplomatic voice. "The crowd seemed to be spitting on us."

"That was venom," said Leeni, the squeaky-voiced one. "It is a biological defense that evolved in the Zhuri's pre-civilized state. It is even more strongly discouraged in our society than smell. But like smell, it can be difficult to control in extreme situations."

"Please forgive our ignorance," Dad said, "but what is 'smell'?"

The Zhuri looked at each other before answering. "Smell is emotion," Leeni explained. "It is how the Zhuri express feeling. When the anger smell becomes strong enough—as it was among the crowd when you arrived—it triggers the release of venom."

So that gasoline smell during the attack was anger. I wondered if the sour-milk stink they were giving off was an emotion too.

"Why were they so angry with us?" Mom asked.

"Because your species is violent," the gruff one explained. "You threaten our peace."

"With all due respect," Mom said, "we are *not* violent."

They both reared their heads back like Mom had just insulted them.

"You destroyed your own planet."

"Other humans did that. Not us. We have learned from the terrible mistakes of others. All the humans who wish to take refuge on Choom are peaceful. We renounce violence and will not harm anyone on your planet."

"Hundreds of Zhuri made strong disagreement all over the shuttle while you were inside," the gruff one said. "If you are so peaceful, why are you not in great fear for your safety?"

"We *are* in great fear," Mom told him. She looked at the rest of us, and we all nodded.

"Our children are terrified, and so are we," Dad said.

The Zhuri looked at each other again.

"But you make no smell," Leeni pointed out.

"Humans do not show emotion through smell," Dad explained.

"Then how do you communicate your emotions to other humans?"

"It shows on our faces, and in our voices."

"So at the moment, you are in fear also?" Leeni asked.

"Yes! Of course," said Mom. "We were just attacked by a swarm of your people."

"That was not a swarm," the gruff one said. "It was an angry gathering."

"What is the difference?" Mom asked.

"A swarm is violent."

"How does it get more violent than that?" Ila yelped.

Mom clicked off her translator and turned to my sister. "Ila: *Don't talk.*"

"Sorry."

"As I said," the gruff one continued, "we apologize for this disturbance. We are preparing another shuttle to return you to the human ship. It will be ready soon."

Mom looked confused. "Why would we return to the human ship?"

"For your own protection," he said. "As you have seen, your presence causes strong disagreement. For your own safety, surely you do not wish to stay?"

"We very much wish to stay," Mom told him. "As we have told you many times, there is nowhere else for us to go."

The Zhuri looked at each other again. "But everyone agrees it is best if you leave," said Leeni. "The emotions you have created make it too dangerous for you to live on Choom."

"With all respect, we did nothing to create those emotions. All we did was step off the ship. Our only wish is to live here in peace. If you give us the chance, we will prove this by our actions."

The two Zhuri leaned their heads toward each other and began to whisper in voices that were too low for our translators to pick up. As they did, the sour-milk smell, which had been fading away, spiked up again. Leeni began to rub her wings together in a strange, awkward movement.

Finally they turned back to us.

"We will discuss this with others and return shortly," the gruff voice said.

The two of them walked in their bendy-legged way to a door and exited through it, leaving us surrounded by the six Zhuri soldiers. Whatever the sour-milk smell was, it disappeared along with the unarmed officials.

"Hello," Mom said to the nearest soldiers.

They didn't answer.

"My name is Amora," she said. "May I ask what your names are?"

The soldiers said nothing. They just kept staring, their weapons pointed right at us.

Eventually we got the hint. The four of us went back inside the shuttle to sit and wonder what the heck was happening.

"What do you think that sour-milk smell was?" I asked.

"Bureaucracy," Dad answered.

I knew that was a joke, but I didn't get it. "What do you mean?"

"He means," Mom said with a sigh, "that those two didn't have the authority to make a decision about us. So they went to find someone who does."

6

A HOME FOR
GIANT MARSHMALLOWS

WE WOUND UP sitting in the shuttle until the middle of the night.

Early on, we got hungry, so Dad opened a container of Chow. I'd been hoping that once we got to Choom, I'd never have to eat it again. But getting attacked by venom-spitting aliens (no, sorry, *we* were the aliens, according to Dad) had left me too hungry to pass it up. I forced down a slice of Barfing while Ila and Mom ate some Choking. Dad had Heaving, which he always picked even though it was the worst flavor by a long shot. I'm pretty sure he ate it out of guilt for having helped create the stuff.

After a while, we all had to go to the bathroom. But the Zhuri ship didn't have one, and when we asked the soldiers if there was one in the hangar, they just stared at us. In a weird way, I was grateful for the distraction. Until my bladder filled up, my mind wouldn't stop racing with the same question, over and over: *How can we live on a planet where swarms of people spit venom at us just for being here?* The worse I had to pee, the harder it was to focus on being scared out of my mind.

For a while, Ila and I tried to take our minds off of our bladders by watching the *Birdleys* episodes we'd brought along. After we went through all the ones on our screens, I tried to download more from the library up on the transport, but I couldn't make a data connection.

"The ship's in orbit on the far side of the planet," Dad explained. "We can't get a signal until it comes around again."

"How long will that take?"

He checked his own screen. "An hour, maybe?"

"Just try to get some sleep," Mom said. "Isn't this gravity making you tired?"

"Tired" wasn't quite the right word. It felt like my flesh was drooping off my skeleton. I lay down on the floor of the shuttle, but it was hard and uncomfortable, and I worried that if I fell asleep, I'd wet my pants.

Finally Leeni came back for us. "I will be your guide until you return to the human ship," she said. "The Immigration Division has found you temporary housing, where you may stay until you leave our planet."

Mom didn't bother explaining again that we couldn't leave because we had nowhere else to go.

Leeni and four of the armed guards got into the shuttle with us, and we flew out of the hangar and across the city. Mom sat in the front row with Leeni. Ila and I were behind them. Dad got stuck in back with the guards.

The sour-milk smell had returned when Leeni did. It was clearly coming from her.

"I have noticed," Mom said, trying to pick her words very carefully, "that there is a smell. Is it caused by an emotion?"

I saw the top of Leeni's head rear back when she heard the translation.

"It is not polite to point out another's smell when they are attempting to control it but cannot," she said.

"I'm so sorry!" Mom said quickly. "I did not mean to offend you."

"I am making a great effort to control my fear smell. It is difficult in your presence."

On top of the sour-milk smell of fear coming from Leeni, I caught a little whiff of gasoline anger. That seemed to be coming from the soldiers behind me. They must not have liked the way Mom was questioning Leeni.

"Please do not be afraid of us," Mom said to Leeni in a gentle voice. "We are peaceful. We would never do anything to hurt you."

"Thank you for saying that," she replied.

Nobody spoke for the rest of the trip. By the time we got where we were going, both the fear and the anger smells had faded away.

We touched down in a little subdivision of a dozen identical honeycomb-shaped houses, all arranged in a six-sided ring around a wide lawn. The shuttle landed on the lawn's edge, and Leeni led us through the moonlight—which was much brighter than on Earth, because Choom had three moons—to the nearest house.

Like all the others in the ring, it was dark, empty-looking, and a single story tall, although that one story was at least as high as a two-story building would've been on Earth.

"These houses were built for Ororo, so their features are quite large," Leeni said, and she wasn't kidding. The front door was wide enough to drive a truck through. Or a six-foot-tall marsh-mallow, which I guess was the point.

We stepped inside, onto a spongy floor that reminded me of kiddie playgrounds back on Earth. There were three bedrooms connected by large doors to the big main room, which had what looked like a giant couch at one end and an equally giant (but very low) table in the middle surrounded by chairs as wide as park benches. At the back end of the main room was a wall of machinery and countertops that looked like a kitchen.

The room we were all desperate to find was in the far right corner.

"The Ororo make body garbage in the same way humans do," Leeni said, pointing to the bathroom door. "You may put yours in the container inside that room."

"First!" Ila yelled as she ran to it, slamming the door behind her. I lined up to go next.

"Hurry up, Ila!"

"Do the Zhuri not make . . . 'body garbage'?" Dad asked Leeni.

"Our waste products leave our bodies as sweat," she told him. "Biologically, this is much more efficient."

Also much more gross, I thought as I heard Ila yell from the other side of the door:

"OHMYGOSH, THIS THING IS ENORMOUS!"

A moment later, there was a noise from the bathroom like a rocket engine.

"Everything okay in there?" Mom called out.

Ila emerged, shaking her head. "Don't sit on it when you flush," she told me. "It'll kill you."

She was right. The toilet was practically hot tub–size, and just low enough for a human to perch on its edge. When I pressed the flush button, the whole thing rose up two feet, shrank to a third its normal width (which was still about five times too wide for a human to sit on), and created a noisy suction so strong that I could feel the air getting sucked into the bowl from halfway across the room.

I managed to use it without dying. After Mom and Dad took their turns, Leeni said goodbye to us.

"I will return in the morning, and we can discuss when you will be leaving," she said hopefully.

After Leeni left, we picked bedrooms. They were all huge, each one several times the size of our whole living compartment on Mars. Mine had a gigantic (but very low) bed and several sets of drawers along the wall, although I didn't have anything to put in them except my spare set of clothes and my screen.

I lay down on the bed to test it. The mattress was made of either very thick liquid or very soft plastic—it rippled out, then reshaped itself around me in a way that was so weird and un-settling, I wondered for a moment if I should just sleep on the floor instead.

But once the mattress finished adapting to my body, I felt like it was giving me a warm hug. It was so comfortable that I fell asleep without even lifting my head.

WHEN I WOKE up, sunlight was streaming through the window. Still groggy, I shut my eyes against the light, but then a thought jolted them open again:

I'm on another planet. And my bed is hugging me.

A second thought forced me up and out of the ridiculously cozy mattress:

I can go outside!

Other than the horrifying few seconds on the tarmac of the spaceport, and the short walk in the darkness from the shuttle to our front door, I hadn't been outside since we left Earth.

I went to the living room. Nobody else was up yet. I looked out the front window. The red lawn was empty.

I tiptoed to the door and opened it. It was quiet and peaceful in our subdivision, with a forest-like smell that was really pleasant. The sun was just above the houses on the far side of the ring, and it felt warm on my face.

I took a step outside, and a pair of pronged weapons came out of nowhere to block my path. Two soldiers had been standing guard against the wall on either side of the front door.

I gasped in fear as one of them whined at me.

"Reeeeyeeeeeeh?"

I jumped back inside and slammed the door. Then I fetched my screen and tried again. This time, I stood in the doorway and tried to be polite.

"Good morning, sirs," I said through my translator, hoping they were sirs and not madams, or maybe another option I didn't even know about.

"Reeeeyeeeeeeh?"

"Where are you going?" the soldier was asking me. I got a whiff of sour-milk fear from one, or maybe both, of them.

"I just want to breathe the air and walk on the grass. Is that okay?"

They looked at each other. "Yes. But do not touch the fence."

I stepped outside and looked around. "Where *is* the fence, sir?"

Instead of answering, the soldier flew straight up into the air, holding his weapon extended above him. Thirty yards up, the tip of the prong hit the fence, and a blue dome of electricity crackled to life around the perimeter of the subdivision.

"Thank you, sir!" I said with a big, friendly smile when he flitted back to the ground.

He didn't answer me. I looked around some more. There was no sign of life in the dozen other houses around the big lawn, and no other structures except for a pill-shaped beige pod about the size of a small car, parked by the side of our house. I figured the pod belonged to the guards.

"Excuse me, but can I ask—does anyone live in these other houses?"

"No," one of the soldiers replied.

"Did anyone ever live there?"

He didn't answer. I walked away from the house toward the middle of the lawn. My bare feet on the red grass felt so good that it almost made me cry. The air smelled delicious, and I sucked in big lungfuls of it.

I knelt down and said a prayer of thanks for the sweet-smelling air, the warm sun, and the quiet peaceful lawn. For a long time, I'd wondered if I'd ever get to enjoy things like that again.

Then I thought about the swarm of Zhuri back at the spaceport, and my heart started to race.

I lay down on the grass and stretched out on my back with my knees bent, taking deep breaths to calm down as I stared up at the green sky.

How great would this place be if the people here didn't spit venom at us?

And those houses were full of humans? And Naya lived next door?

I swore to myself that I was going to help make all of that happen. I was going to be the best, friendliest, most awesome human I could be. I was going to change all their minds about us.

Ruff, ruff.

Then there was a crackling thunderclap, and the electric fence lit up.

I sat up, my heart racing again. A pill-shaped beige pod had crossed the fence above the houses on the far side of the subdivision. It was flying straight at me.

By the time it landed on the lawn in front of the house, I was back inside with the door shut. Mom and Dad were just coming out of their bedroom, looking half-asleep. The noise from the fence must have woken them up.

Dad went to the window. "I think it's Leeni," he said.

It was. She was carrying two large containers. "I thought you would be interested to try the foods of our different species," she told us.

Ila's bedroom door flew open. "Did I hear the word 'food'?"

Leeni put four glasses on the low table and poured thick, gray liquid into each one for us to drink.

"This is Zhuri food."

It smelled like dirty gym socks, and it tasted even worse.

"Are there other flavors?" Mom asked, trying to be polite.

"No," said Leeni. "We have never understood why food should come in more than one flavor. Everyone agrees it is not efficient."

Next up was the Krik food. It was also disgusting, but in a completely different way: it wouldn't stop wriggling.

"When the Zhuri first came to Planet Choom," Leeni explained, "the Krik who lived here ate small animals, which they consumed while they were still alive."

She set down a rectangular container of Krik food, and it rattled around on the table like a jumping bean.

Mom gasped. "There's a live animal in there?"

"No. We found the Krik's eating habits barbaric, so we helped them genetically engineer the *yeero* plant to move in ways that remind them of their former prey."

Leeni opened the container, took out the yeero, and put it on a plate. It looked like a medium-sized cucumber, but with a couple dozen wriggling tentacles sprouting from it on all sides.

"That's a *vegetable*?" Ila's face was pale.

"Does it die when you cut into it?" Dad asked.

"Technically speaking," said Leeni, "it is already dead." She cut it into four pieces with a knife, and they all kept flopping around just as frantically as before.

"I think we would prefer not to eat that," Mom said politely.

"A wise choice," said Leeni. "When eaten, it does not stop moving in the stomach for some time."

"Is that everything?" Ila asked.

"No," said Leeni, reaching into her shopping bag for more containers. "There is also Ororo food. It comes in a frankly ridiculous number of flavors, but I have brought only the five most common. I doubt you will enjoy them."

After striking out with the Zhuri and Krik samples, we didn't have much hope left. But the Ororo stuff was incredible. Each type was a brightly colored, perfectly square block that had its own specific flavor and texture. The flavors were all over the place—savory, sweet, bitter, and a couple I didn't even have words for—and so were their textures. Some were crisp, some were chewy, and there was a purple one that melted almost instantly in my mouth.

All five of them tasted amazing. Between the four of us, we ate every last bite in just a couple of minutes.

"That. Was. Phenomenal," said Ila when it was gone.

"It is curious that you prefer Ororo food," said Leeni. "It is so much less efficient than the others."

"Leeni, we are very grateful you brought this to us!" said Mom with a big smile. "It is so kind of you!" The rest of us took the hint, thanking Leeni with gushing words and big, goofy grins. I worried we were laying it on a little too thick, but Leeni seemed to appreciate it.

"I am glad you enjoyed the food," she told us. "Have you decided yet when you will leave our planet?"

Mom didn't let her smile slip. "Why do you wish for us to leave?"

"Everyone agrees it is best for both your safety and ours if you do not stay on Choom. The human history of violence has caused great emotion among our people."

"You have spent some time with us now. Do we seem violent to you?"

"You do not," Leeni admitted. "Even so, you are the cause of much disagreement. Everyone agrees it is better if you do not stay."

"We are very peaceful," Mom promised. "There is nothing to

fear from us. And we very much wish to stay here. My husband and I are eager to take jobs and contribute to Choom's society. Our children want to attend school. Before we arrived, the Unified Government promised us the chance to do these things."

A hint of sour milk drifted over from Leeni's side of the table. "This is true," she admitted. "But after yesterday's disturbance, everyone agrees it is no longer wise. The Executive Division has ruled that you may not leave this subdivision except to return to the spaceport and fly back to the human ship."

"May I ask who made that ruling?" Mom said in a polite voice.

"Everyone agrees it is best."

"I understand that. But someone must have issued the order. Who decided we cannot leave this house?"

Leeni rubbed her wings together awkwardly. "The chief servant of the Executive Division."

"May we meet with this chief servant?"

"I can request a videoconference with him."

"We would prefer to meet in person."

Leeni rubbed her wings together again, like it was some kind of nervous tic. "I do not see how this is possible. The Executive Division is on the other side of the city. You are not allowed to travel there."

"Would the chief servant travel to us?"

Leeni stared at Mom like she didn't understand the question. Mom smiled even bigger than before.

"On the human planet," she told Leeni, "we have a custom. It is much honored, and of great importance. It is called a dinner party. We humbly ask that the chief servant come here and join us in observing it. We also welcome any other Zhuri who wish to attend, along with representatives of Choom's other species. We would very much like to meet them all."

"What would be the purpose of this 'dinner party' custom?" Leeni asked.

"To introduce ourselves. And to show the chief servant that the people of Choom have nothing to fear from humans."

More wing rubbing. "I will inform the Executive Division of your request," said Leeni.

A FEW MINUTES later, the four of us stood on the lawn, watching Leeni's pod fly away.

"Let's all pray this chief servant says yes," Mom said.

"If we have a dinner party," I piped up, "can we ask the Ororo to bring the food?"

"No way," Dad said. "We're serving Chow."

"Dad!"

"Kidding! Geez."

"If they say yes," Mom told me, "I will personally get on my knees and *beg* them to bring more of that Ororo food."

Dad scowled. "Chow kept a lot of people alive, you know."

Mom put her arm around him. "I know, honey. We're very grateful. But we're not serving it to guests."

7

ALIEN DINNER PARTY

IT TOOK MORE than a day, but the chief servant of the Executive Division (whatever that was) finally accepted Mom's invitation. The next evening, we hosted the Most Important Dinner Party in Human History.

Or at least it was the Most Important Dinner Party Not Held on Earth.

Our guests were five giant mosquitoes, one little green werewolf, and a six-foot-tall marshmallow with arms.

Four Zhuri soldiers came too, but they weren't there to eat. They were just there to electrocute us if we did anything violent.

Another three Zhuri showed up early to set up the food, which we were thrilled to see included enough Ororo rations for the humans too. One of the Zhuri also brought video cameras—three baseball-sized drones that floated in the air, recording everything we did.

"May I ask what those are for?" Mom said to the Zhuri worker who was launching them.

"They will record footage for Choom's television news."

"Choom has television?"

It was our first inkling that there was TV on the planet. But the workers ignored all our questions about it, no matter how politely we asked or how much we smiled when we did.

The five Zhuri guests were Leeni, the gruff-sounding official who'd been with her in the spaceport hangar, the chief servant—who looked much older than the others, with dead spots in his compound eyes and his greenish-brown skin faded almost to gray—and two Zhuri who were shorter than the rest.

The short ones turned out to be kids.

"My name is Hooree," the smallest one announced, standing opposite me. "I was hatched at a similar time as you." The translator app gave her a pinched, crabby-sounding older lady's voice.

"Hello, Hooree!" I said with my biggest smile, hoping the Zhuri knew that human smiles were meant to be friendly. "My name is Lan! I am very happy to meet you!"

The smile didn't seem to help. Hooree reeked of sour-milk fear.

"I am Iruu," the second-shortest one told Ila. His voice sounded so much like a cartoon frog that I almost giggled at the sound of it. "I am also very close to your biological age."

"I'm Ila," my sister told him, trying to smile but not really pulling it off. In the two days we'd been on the planet, she'd been acting even more withdrawn and depressed than she was on Mars. The only time her gloom had lifted for even a few minutes was when Leeni had fed us the Ororo food. "It is nice to meet you."

"We have asked Hooree and Iruu to attend this meal as company for the younger humans," Leeni explained, "and to help us determine how well they might fit in at a Choom school."

57

"Thank you so much for coming!" I beamed at the Zhuri kids. "We are very honored to have you!"

All I got in reply was more fear stink from Hooree.

After that, Leeni introduced the Ororo and the Krik to us. They were both government officials of some kind.

"We apologize that our translators cannot yet convert your speech into a form we understand," Mom told the giant marshmallow and the little green werewolf.

"*MRRRRRMMMMMM*," rumbled the big Ororo in reply.

We all looked to Leeni for a translation, but she didn't offer one. Eventually Mom stopped waiting and changed the subject.

"Was no one from the Nug species able to attend?" Mom asked. "We had looked forward to meeting them as well."

At the mention of the Nug, the Zhuri adults all rubbed their wings together in the nervous-looking way we'd seen Leeni do before. The little Krik snapped her razor-toothed mouth open and shut, and the Ororo's thick eyelids lowered in a way that looked sad.

"There are no longer Nug on Planet Choom," Leeni explained.

"I am so sorry," Mom said. "I did not know that."

There was an awkward silence.

"Perhaps the children would like to go outside and make sport," Leeni suggested.

Iruu, the older one, held up a curved disc that looked like a Frisbee. "I have brought a *suswut* disc! Do you wish to learn how to play?"

"We would love to do this!" I said cheerfully. As I started toward the door, I heard Ila groan. Back on Earth, she'd never been much for sports.

When we walked out the door with the two Zhuri kids, a pair of the armed guards went with us. I guess they weren't taking any chances.

In the time it took us to walk out to the middle of the big red lawn, I cooked up a whole fantasy in my head that I'd somehow become the greatest suswut player Choom had ever seen. My amazing athletic skills would win over the entire planet, and they'd let the rest of the humans come to Choom in the hope of finding more suswut stars like me.

The fantasy lasted until Hooree and Iruu took to the air, flying straight up to hover ten feet over our heads. Iruu tossed the suswut disc at Hooree, who caught it and then looked down at us.

"Can you fly?" she asked.

"I'm so sorry!" I told her. "Humans can't fly."

"Oh." The two of them slowly sank back to the ground.

"If you cannot fly, you will not be good at suswut," said Iruu, hanging his head in a way that made me think he was really disappointed.

"Can we try anyway?" I asked.

Hooree shook her head. "It will not be fun. Krik and Ororo cannot fly either. They are both terrible at suswut." She sounded mean and snotty, and I wondered if it was because of her personality, or just her angry-grandmother voice signature.

One of the baseball-sized camera drones was hovering at eye level a couple of feet away from us, its glittering lens pointed straight at me. I tried to keep the goofy grin on my face, but it was starting to make my face hurt.

We stood there, nobody saying anything and Hooree silently

reeking of fear, until I finally blurted out, "Thank you again for coming to this dinner! We are very grateful for your kindness!"

"It was not our choice," said Hooree. "We were ordered to come here."

"Leeni told us to come," Iruu added, sounding a lot friendlier than his partner. "We live in his hive."

"Wait—is Leeni a 'him'?" I asked. I'd been calling him "her" because of his squeaky-little-girl voice signature.

"I do not understand your question," said Hooree.

"It's like . . . in humans, there are mostly males and females," I explained. "Males are 'he,' and females are 'she.' And, um . . ."

Iruu nodded. "When the male and the female mate, you reproduce, yes? The Ororo and Krik are also this way. But the Zhuri are not. Only our regents are female. The regents lay all the eggs for the hive. The rest of us are male."

"That is *very* interesting!" I said. "Isn't it, Ila?"

"Mmmm." My sister had given up even trying to smile.

There was another awkward silence.

"How many people are in your hive?" I asked the Zhuri.

"Three thousand four hundred and seventeen," said Hooree.

"That is a lot of people!" I said. "Is there a long line for the bathroom in the morning?"

Hooree and Iruu just stared at me. Then I remembered the Zhuri didn't go to the bathroom.

"I'm sorry! I was trying to make a joke."

"People should not make jokes," said Hooree. "Everyone agrees jokes are not polite. They cause emotion."

"I'm so sorry!" I repeated as my stomach did a flip-flop. "I didn't know that."

"It is true jokes are not polite," said Iruu. "But some people think it is all right to make them sometimes."

Hooree's head swiveled to stare at the older Zhuri. "Who thinks this?"

"I do not know any of them personally," said Iruu. "But I have heard that some people think this."

"Those people are not correct," Hooree insisted. "Making jokes is *never* all right. Everyone agrees this is true."

I definitely liked Iruu a lot better than Hooree.

"Did Leeni say you go to a school?" I was surprised to hear Ila open her mouth without being told to do it.

"Yes," Iruu replied. "We both attend the Iseeyii Interspecies Academy. It is the school where you would go if you were allowed to attend."

"I would *love* to attend school!" I said, nodding my head excitedly. "I enjoy learning things and meeting new people!"

The Zhuri just stared at me, and I cringed inside. I was trying too hard.

Ila took a deep, shaky breath. "If we went to your school," she asked in a trembling voice, "would the students spit venom on us?"

Both of the Zhuri drew their heads back. "Oh no!" said Iruu. "That would never happen. Making disagreement in that way is *very* bad. No one would ever do that to you."

"They *did* do that to us," Ila said. "When they swarmed us at the spaceport."

"That was not a swarm!" Hooree whined. "It was an angry gathering!"

He and Iruu were both rubbing their wings together, which

by now I'd figured out was Zhuri body language for *This conversation is making us very uncomfortable.*

"What's the difference?"

"If it was a swarm, it would have been much worse," Iruu told me. "But even so, everyone agrees what happened at the spaceport was very bad. And nothing like it would *ever* happen at our school."

"If you are peaceful, there will be no problems," said Hooree. "At Iseeyii, all three species study together without disagreement."

"What happened to the fourth species?" I asked.

"There are only three," Iruu told me. "The Zhuri, the Krik, and the Ororo."

"But when we first talked to people on Choom, there were four. Those three, plus the Nug."

Hooree and Iruu stared at each other. "I have never heard of this species," said Iruu.

"It does not exist," said Hooree.

"It did once," I insisted. "Did you hear the adults? They were just talking about it. And I saw one in a video. It was really big and slippery, with this huge hole for a mouth. It moved like this"— I did my best imitation of a slithering Nug—"and it screeched, like 'SKREEEEEEEEE!'"

Hooree backed away from me in what looked like horror, and his fear smell—which had been gradually fading away—suddenly came back.

But Iruu didn't back away, and I caught a whiff of a different kind of smell coming from him. Unlike the gasoline anger and the sour-milk fear, this one wasn't gross. It was actually pleasant—it had a sweet, almost tasty odor, like a fresh-baked doughnut.

Hooree shook his head. "You are wrong," he told me. "If there was such a species, we would know about it."

"That movement you made is very strange," said Iruu. "Can you make it again?"

Before I could answer either of them, the front door opened. Dad called out:

"Kids! We're sitting down to dinner now."

I TRIED NOT to stare at the yeero plant flopping back and forth under the Krik's hand as she pressed it against her plate to keep it from wriggling across the table. We'd all been served—there were ten different colors of Ororo food arranged in perfect cubes on my plate, and I couldn't wait to dig into them—but we had to wait for the elderly chief servant to finish his speech about how important immigration was to Planet Choom.

All three of the drone cameras fixed their lenses on him from different angles as he spoke:

"Just as the Krik welcomed the Zhuri to Planet Choom one thousand and twelve years ago—and the Zhuri and Krik together invited the Ororo one hundred and ninety-six years ago—our Unified Government welcomes all species who seek refuge here. In return, we insist only that the refugees are peaceful and do not cause disagreement. Today we welcome the Mifune-Persaud human reproductive unit as temporary guests while we consider whether the human species can satisfy these conditions."

Then it was Mom's turn. She stood up, facing the chief servant across the table, and the drone cameras all turned to record her.

"We thank you, from deep in our hearts, for your kindness in welcoming us to Planet Choom. Following the darkest chapter in the history of the human species, your civilization is a light that has drawn us across the galaxy at your invitation. We wish only to live among you in peace, and to contribute in a positive way to Choom's society."

Sitting next to me—the Ororo-sized chairs were so wide that we were sharing one—Ila cleared her throat and shifted nervously. She'd agreed to sing for the group, and her big moment was coming up.

"As an example of the many gifts we have to offer," Mom continued, "my eldest child, Ila, wishes to sing for you. Music is one of many human art forms that—"

"YEEEEEHEEEE—" The chief servant's wings beat rapidly as he rose several inches off his chair, interrupting Mom in a harsh whine.

"TURN OFF THE CAMERAS."

Along the far wall, the Zhuri in charge of the cameras flitted over to the control panel and hit a button. When he did, all three cameras fell from midair, clattering onto the floor.

"I am so sorry!" Mom said quickly. "Have I said something that offends you?"

The chief servant folded his wings, settling back into his seat. But the tone of his whining stayed harsh, and the smell of gasoline spread across the table. "You wish to force *art* upon us? We want nothing to do with art! Not yours, or anyone's! The only purpose of art is emotion—and emotion is poisonous. Choom is a civilized society. We have evolved beyond such barbaric displays."

Mom was so stunned that the smile left her face. "With all due respect," she said, struggling to keep her voice pleasant and cheerful, "we believe some forms of art and emotion are very positive. In some cases, they represent all that is best in a species—"

"Nonsense!"

Mom somehow forced the smile back onto her face. "The Zhuri who first invited us here showed great interest in our art. They wished to—"

The chief servant interrupted again. "Those Zhuri were fools. They no longer lead us. And even they now agree that emotion leads only to chaos. In recent years, we have succeeded in removing all emotion from our society."

The gasoline stink was rolling off him. I wondered how he could possibly say there was no emotion in Choom's society when he reeked of anger himself.

Mom called him on it. She never stopped smiling, but her voice turned hard. "How is it that you claim to be free of emotion when hundreds of your people attacked us in a rage?"

"That was *your* emotion! The human caused that!"

The whine of his voice was getting much louder. Ila grabbed my hand under the table and squeezed it tight. When I glanced at her, she looked as worried as I felt.

"With all respect," Mom replied, lowering and softening her own voice, "we did nothing to cause that. All we did was step off a ship."

"Your very presence caused the emotion! And now you want

us to open our workplaces and schools to you? To stir up still more emotion?"

The smell of anger was coming from more of them than just the chief servant now, and there was fear mixed in with it. I looked around at the Zhuri, wondering if one of them might puke venom on us at any second.

"Your government agreed to this," Mom gently reminded the chief servant. "You invited us across a galaxy to work and study among you. We believe your people's anger and fear is based on misunderstanding. We are only four humans. We have no weapons, and we pose no threat. If you let us enter your schools and workplaces, we believe your people will see for themselves that we are peaceful."

The chief servant stared at Mom with his dead-spotted compound eyes. Then he turned to Hooree and Iruu, sitting on the far side of me.

"What do you say, children? What would you think if these humans attended your school?"

They both started to answer at once.

"I do not think they should—" Hooree began.

"It would be interesting to us!" said Iruu, talking over his classmate. "The presence of a new species would be educational. And the human children are quite weak. They cannot even fly. We are in agreement that they are no threat to us. Aren't we, Hooree?"

"Of course, everyone agrees," said Hooree in a low, defeated-sounding whine.

The chief servant turned to the Krik, who had gotten tired of waiting and had started to eat her wriggling vegetable. Her eyes were on her plate, and she didn't seem to be listening to the conversation anymore.

"From the Krik perspective, what is your opinion about working alongside humans?"

The Krik looked up. Stray bits of tentacle slapped the outside of her mouth. Realizing she was being called on, she quickly swallowed.

"GZZRRRZZKKGZZRK."

Nobody translated the Krik's words for us. But the chief servant reared his head back like the Krik hadn't told him what he wanted to hear. As they watched him, Leeni and the gruff-sounding Zhuri both rubbed their wings together nervously.

"The human has nothing that is useful to us," the chief servant whined. "You are not as strong as the Krik, as clever as the Ororo, or as civilized as the Zhuri. If we allow you into our workplaces and schools, it will only be a waste of everyone's time."

"With all respect," said Mom, "until we try, how can you know for sure? All we ask is that you give us a chance—the same chance you guaranteed us before we crossed the galaxy to come here. If the promises of your government have meaning, we beg you to honor them. Give us a chance."

The old Zhuri picked up the glass of gray liquid that sat in front of him. He stuck his tubelike mouth into it and drained the whole thing with one long suck, making a loud slurpy noise at the end. Then he banged the empty glass down on the table. The anger smell was starting to fade.

"Very well," he said. "The Unified Government honors its agreements, no matter how foolishly they were made. You will be

67

assigned jobs that suit you, and your children may attend school. But everyone agrees this experiment will fail. As soon as it does, you will leave this planet forever."

With that, he stood up and flitted out of the house.

The others followed him, although the Ororo tipped his plate into his mouth and ate his whole meal in one bite before standing up and waddling out. A minute later, the only nonhuman left in the house was Leeni.

"Congratulations," he said. "I will send pods in the morning to take the children to school, and yourselves to your new workplaces."

As I wondered if I should change Leeni's voice signature in my translator to make him sound like a guy now that I knew he was male, Dad piped up. "May I ask a question?"

"Of course. It is my job to answer your questions."

"What did that Krik say about working alongside humans?"

Leeni rubbed his wings. "She said that you seemed quite weak and helpless. And that if either of you caused problems, the Krik working with you could simply bite your heads off."

Dad laughed nervously. "That was a joke, right?"

"It was not. Everyone agrees jokes should not be told. They cause emotion."

My stomach did a flip-flop. For a planet that everybody claimed was peaceful, there seemed to be an awful lot of violence on Choom.

And so far, all of it was aimed at us.

8

WHO WANTS TO EAT THE NEW KID?

"I DON'T WANT to go," Ila told me.

"We *have* to go. And it'll be good! Are you going to finish that purple stuff?" We were sitting at the table, eating Ororo leftovers for breakfast.

"Yes! Don't touch it!" The purple stuff was everybody's favorite.

My sister looked over to make sure Mom was still in the bathroom and couldn't hear us, then shook her head. "It's never going to work," she said in a quiet voice. "They don't want us here."

"Some of them do," I told her. "Those Zhuri kids yesterday were nice. One of them was, anyway. And we can win the rest of them over. We just have to be awesome."

"What happens when they freak out and spit venom on us?"

"They won't! They promised that wouldn't happen at this school."

"We got promised a lot of things that didn't happen," Ila muttered.

"Will you stop being so negative?" My sister was really getting on my nerves. I was plenty worried about going to school myself, but I felt like I couldn't even mention it, because I'd just be giving her *we're all doomed* act more ammunition.

Ila opened her mouth to fire back, but then Dad came out of the bedroom, and she held off. Like all of us, Dad had two sets of clothes. Unlike Ila and me, today he was wearing his more casual one—a faded blue T-shirt and a pair of cargo shorts.

"Why the long faces? This is a big day!"

"Why aren't you wearing your good clothes?" Ila asked.

"Because I got the sense they're not exactly putting us in office jobs," he said. "Besides, the Zhuri don't wear clothes at all. They're not going to get on my case for being underdressed. Is there any purple stuff left?"

"Sorry, Dad."

"Oh, come on!"

"There's yellow stuff."

"That's almost as good. We've got to figure out how to get more of this food."

I thought about making a Chow joke, but Dad was in a good mood, and I didn't want to spoil it.

TWO PODS CAME at the same time, announcing their arrival with the usual thunderclap of the fence getting breached.

"What's the point of having a fence if people can just fly through it?" I asked.

"They can't," Dad explained. "According to Leeni, the pods need some kind of clearance code to get through. Otherwise the fence will shut down their electrical systems, and they'll crash."

Both of the pods were autopiloted, and they each had a pair of armed Zhuri soldiers waiting inside. Mom and Dad hugged us goodbye and reminded us to be our happiest, friendliest selves. Then Ila and I got into our pod. The interior was bland, plastic, and mostly empty, with benches along the walls that reminded me of a monorail I'd taken at an Earth airport once.

Ila and I said cheerful hellos to the two soldiers. They just stared at us in response, but I was relieved to see that my sister was at least trying to be friendly to the Zhuri. Then we flew off to school.

The flight took about fifteen minutes. Our subdivision must have been on the outskirts of the city, because when we started flying, there were lots of red lawns in between all the honeycomb-shaped beige buildings. As we kept going, the lawns got fewer and farther between, until finally there was almost no open ground anywhere. It was all low beige buildings, as far as we could see.

But then another red lawn came into view among the buildings, this one as big as a football field. Next to it was an equally huge three-story building. Our pod started to descend toward the big building, and there was a familiar, hair-raising *BZZZZZT!* as we passed through an electrical fence. It lit up in a blue half sphere that covered both the building and the giant field next to it.

After the fence lit up, there was a sudden blur of movement along one of the pathways just outside it, and I heard a familiar-sounding whine that made my stomach drop.

It was a swarm of Zhuri—or an "angry gathering," whatever that meant. Our translators were already on in case the soldiers wanted to talk to us, and mine converted the crowd's chant right away:

"HUMANS GO HOME! HUMANS GO HOME!"

"Oh no, no, no . . ." Ila put her hand over her eyes. "Not again—"

"It's okay," I said. "They're on the other side of the fence."

"The fences break!"

"This one won't break," I said, even though I had no idea if it was true. "We'll be fine."

Our translators had converted the whole conversation for the soldiers to hear. One of them finally spoke.

"The fence will not break," he said. "The gathering is very small."

"See?" I told my sister. She just shook her head and grimaced.

There were at least a hundred Zhuri, but they weren't as riled up as the ones at the airport, because none of them hit the screen and got zapped as we stepped out of the pod and walked to the building. Even so, their shrieks were so loud and angry that I felt shaky with fear as we approached the huge front door, where three Zhuri were waiting for us.

Two of them turned out to be Hooree and Iruu. The third, much taller one introduced himself as "Hiyew, the chief educator of the Iseeyii Interspecies Academy." I figured that meant he was the principal.

"Welcome," the principal said over the shrieks of the protestors. "The mission of Iseeyii is to promote peace and agreement among all species. We are eager to have the human join us. Please, come inside."

After Ila and I gushed our thanks, and I smiled so big that I practically sprained a muscle in my cheek, we followed him into the building.

The armed soldiers walked in behind us. They stood just a couple of feet from Ila and me, prong weapons at their sides, as the principal pointed out his office just off the big honeycomb-shaped lobby.

"Hooree and Iruu will be your guides until you no longer need them," he said. "If you have problems they cannot solve, please come to my office. I will be happy to help you at any time. Everyone agrees you are valued members of our community, and some people think you may contribute greatly to our common education. Do you have questions?"

"No, sir," said Ila.

"No, sir!" I chimed in. "Thank you! We are very excited to learn, and to meet our fellow students!"

I cringed a little inside after I said it. There was a fine line between incredibly friendly and just plain annoying, and I was pretty sure I'd landed on the wrong side of it. But the principal just nodded.

"I am very glad to hear this. Iruu and Hooree will escort you to your classes now. They have already begun, so you should go quickly."

"Yes, sir! Thank you!"

"Thank you, sir."

"I'll see you soon," I told Ila as I gave her an awkward goodbye hug. We'd never really been the hugging types, but she looked like she needed it—and even though she stiffened up for an instant, she quickly relaxed and hugged me back. Then she followed Iruu down one of the two wide hallways leading out of the lobby, while I went with Hooree down the other.

The soldiers split up, with one following each of us. Apparently, we were going to have bodyguards while we were in school. I wondered if they were supposed to protect us from the Zhuri, or to protect the Zhuri from us.

The hallway was open all the way to the skylit roof, three stories above. On the upper two floors, I saw narrow hallways on each side, lined with honeycomb-shaped doors to what I guessed were classrooms. The place might have reminded me of a shopping mall, but with an armed guard at my heels, it seemed more like a prison.

I had to practically run to keep up with Hooree. His wings were flitting in a sort of half walk, half fly.

"This is a very nice school!" I told him.

"Please move faster," he said in his crabby-old-lady voice. "Our class has started."

Two-thirds of the way down the hall, he stopped at a door and led me inside.

I wound up in the back corner of a room full of about thirty students, all sitting on stools and holding screens. Most of them were Zhuri, but along the back wall, five Krik sat in a row.

The Zhuri teacher stood at the front of the room, using some kind of laser marker to add to a jumble of unreadable writing on a big wall-mounted screen. When he saw us enter, he stopped writing.

"Welcome to Education Room Six None Six," he said. "I am Learning Specialist Yurinuri. Please, human—sit down."

"Thank you, sir!"

I looked around for a seat. Hooree had already taken one, blending into the group so fast that I was no longer sure which one he was. The soldier stood against the wall next to the door. I only saw one empty stool, near the middle of the room.

I walked over to it, trying to ignore the stink of fear rising up from my new classmates. When I sat down, I heard the *skrrrrtch* of stool legs scraping the floor as they all tried to move as far away from me as possible.

By the time they stopped, there was about six feet of no-man's-land surrounding me in every direction, and the rest of the class was crammed elbow to elbow along the walls.

The sour-milk smell was getting heavier by the second. So far, this wasn't going very well.

Yurinuri stared at me with his unblinking eyes. "How do you wish to be called, human?"

It took me a second to understand what he was asking. "My name is Lan Mifune!" I told him, grinning like an idiot.

"Lan Mifune. Very good: Room Six None Six, please welcome the Lan Mifune to our group."

"WELCOME, THE LAN MIFUNE," everybody said.

"Please, Room Six None Six—clear the air of your smell. Everyone agrees there is nothing to fear from the Lan Mifune. Move back into the middle of the room." Yurinuri gestured with his hands for the Zhuri kids to get closer to me.

There was a lot *skrrrtch*-ing as everybody made a show of pushing their stools closer. But by the time they were finished, I still had several feet of empty space around me.

Yurinuri's head swiveled as he looked around the class. "I

think it is best," he said, "if we give the Lan Mifune a chance to tell us more about itself. Since none of us has ever seen a human except on our television screens, I am sure we have many questions for it. Lan Mifune, do you agree to this?"

"Okay," I said.

"Good." He beckoned to me with his long, sticklike arm. "Please come to the front of the room."

I got up and walked over to stand next to him, facing the class. The group was shaped like a horseshoe, with the Zhuri in two thick clumps on either side and the Krik along the back wall. My stool sat alone in the empty center of the horseshoe.

"Tell us about yourself," Yurinuri told me.

They all stared at me with their alien eyes: the Zhuri's huge and unblinking, the Krik's red and fierce. My stomach felt like there was a black hole in it, sucking up all my energy.

"My name is Lan," I said, trying to smile through my fear. "I used to live on a planet called Earth. But humans can't live there anymore. So we're, um, hoping we can live on Choom. We are very peaceful! And we, um, want to agree with you!"

The Zhuri seemed big on "agreement," so I figured I'd throw it in. After that, I didn't know what else to say.

I was also getting dizzy, because I'd forgotten to breathe. I tried to smile while I took a few deep breaths.

There was a long, uncomfortable silence.

Finally the teacher rescued me. "Does anyone have questions for the Lan?" he asked. "I am sure you all want to know more about the human."

One of the Krik at the back of the room raised his hand.

I pointed to her. *"RZZZRR GRZZZZR?"* she growled as my translator beeped the "unknown language" warning.

"Arkzer, that question is not appropriate," Yurinuri scolded the Krik.

"I'm sorry," I said. "My translator doesn't understand Krik accents. What was the question?"

"It is not important," Yurinuri said.

"I'm happy to answer anything!" I said, trying to seem cheerful.

"She asked what you tasted like."

Oh geez. The Krik who'd asked the question had teeth like razors, and she seemed to be drooling with hunger. My heart started to race even faster.

"Oh! Wow. I do *not* taste good. Definitely not. Especially my feet. Like, these shoes I'm wearing? They belonged to, like, five other people before me. And they smell horrible. So do my feet. So . . . yeah. Not good eating. At all."

I was trying to be funny. Then I remembered the Zhuri didn't like jokes.

Oh geez.

"I have a question," Yurinuri said. "The part of you that smells bad and is not yours—what was that word again?"

"My shoes?"

"Yes. What are shoes?"

"Oh!" I pointed to my dirty blue running shoes. I'd gotten them from the clothing exchange, and they were so old that the soles were coming apart. "These are shoes. They're like clothing for your feet."

"Do all humans wear shoes?" Yurinuri asked.

"Most of them."

A Zhuri kid raised his hand. "What is clothing?"

"Oh—it's, um, the things we wear on our bodies." I plucked at my shirt and pants to illustrate. "Like, this is clothing."

"Do all humans wear clothing?"

"Most of the time, yeah."

"Why?"

"They, um, keep us warm. And we like to cover our . . . private parts. And, uh, we think it looks good."

"It does not look good," the Zhuri kid told me.

"Oh. Okay! Thank you for your feedback!"

Several hands had gone up. I pointed to one of them.

"How do you make your body garbage?"

Oh geez. I didn't expect that to come up.

"We have, uh . . . holes. Down below. Like I think the Ororo do? And maybe the Krik have them too?"

Another hand. "Can we see the holes?"

My face turned hot. "No! I'm sorry. That's kind of why we wear clothes. Because humans don't like to, um . . . it's private. Do you have privacy? Do you know what I mean by that?"

They looked at each other and whispered.

"We have secrets," says Yurinuri. "Is that what you mean?"

"Kind of? But it's, um . . . it's different. Never mind!" I tried to remember to smile.

Another hand went up. The Zhuri pointed between his eyes. "Are the holes in your face for body garbage?"

"What? No . . ." I pointed to my nose. "These are for smelling things."

"Is that also how you make smell?"

"We don't really make smell. Except . . ." For a moment, I wondered if I should explain farting. Then I decided that was probably a bad idea. "Um, no. We don't."

"You do not have a smell gland?"

"No. We don't make smell. Not on purpose."

They looked at each other and whispered.

"Students . . . ," Yurinuri warned. "Remember your manners."

Another hand went up. "If you do not make smell, how do other humans know when you are having feelings?"

"They can see by our faces. Like, when we're happy, we smile." I gave them the biggest grin I could manage. "Or we just tell people how we feel. Like, we'll say, 'I'm sad.'"

"The Krik and Ororo also use facial expressions in this way," Yurinuri reminded the Zhuri kids, gesturing toward the cluster of Krik students in the back. A few of the Krik nodded, but it didn't seem to make me any less strange to the Zhuri kids. They were still staring at each other and muttering as they shook their heads.

One of the Krik had his hand up. *"BZZRLZRRR?"*

I looked at Yurinuri.

"What do you eat?" he translated.

"Oh! We used to eat a lot of different things," I tell the Krik. "But lately we've just, um, been eating this one thing? Because we ran out of everything else. But—oh! We *love* Ororo food!"

The Zhuri all drew their heads back like they were disgusted. All five of the Krik had their hands up. As I called on them, Yurinuri translated.

"GZZRREE?"

"Is the thing you eat alive?"

"No."

"HRRZZZRR?"

"Is it an animal?"

"No."

"HRZR MZZRZR?"

"Do you eat Ororo?"

"No!"

"MRRRZZR HHRR?"

"Do you eat other humans?"

"No! We definitely do *not* eat other humans." The Krik were all waving their hands in the air. It was a little terrifying how interested they were in talking about eating people. I glanced over at the soldier near the door, hoping he was close enough to step in if somebody tried to eat me.

He didn't seem to be paying much attention. Fortunately, there was a Zhuri in the front row with his hand up, so I called on him next instead of another Krik.

"Hi! Yes . . . ?"

"Why do you kill other humans?"

The question felt like a punch in the stomach.

"I don't," I said. "I've never killed anybody."

"But all humans kill," the Zhuri kid said.

"No, they don't."

The sour-milk smell of fear was spiking up again.

"Yes, they do. I have seen it on television."

I could feel myself getting shaky. "No," I said. "Most humans are peaceful."

I tried to smile, but my face wouldn't cooperate.

Another hand went up. "How can you be peaceful when you destroyed your whole planet?"

"I didn't—it wasn't us! It was just a few bad people." There was a lump rising in my throat. I hadn't cried about Earth in ages, and I definitely didn't want to start again now.

"Why did you let them do it?"

"We didn't—they just—they had powerful weapons, and—"

I stopped in mid-sentence and took a deep breath, trying to hold back the tears.

Half the hands in the room were up now, and they all reeked of fear.

Not just fear. I smelled anger too.

"Children!" Yurinuri whined. "Clear the air! Everyone agrees there is no place for smell in this class."

But the smell stayed, and the questions kept coming. "Did you bring your explosion weapons to our planet?"

"No! We don't have any weapons! We're peaceful!"

"When you lived on Earth, how many humans did you kill?"

I started to cry. I really, really didn't want to. I couldn't help it.

"I've never killed anyone!" I used the back of my hand to wipe the tears off my cheeks. "I've never *hurt* anyone. I'm peaceful! Humans are peaceful."

"Children! Clear the air! Please!" Yurinuri scolded them. I looked over at him, my eyes begging for help.

"You seem to be a peaceful human," he said. "When the other humans tried to kill you, how did you defend yourself?"

"No one—they didn't—everyone who's left is—" My mind

81

suddenly flashed back to the food riot on Mars, when the angry mob showed up outside our living compartment and tried to bust down our door.

That opened the floodgates. I started to sob.

Quit crying! Get a grip! Make them like you!

I couldn't help it. I was coming apart.

"Perhaps you should sit down now," Yurinuri told me.

I stumbled back to my seat. My nose was running, I was still ugly-crying, and I had to wipe my nose with the bottom of my shirt, because I didn't have anything else. As Yurinuri returned to the lesson he was teaching when we first walked in, I heard two kids whisper to each other somewhere off to my left:

"Look at the liquid on its face."

"Is *that* how it makes its body garbage?"

SHAKEDOWN IN
THE LUNCHROOM

AFTER I MANAGED to quit bawling, everybody ignored me for the rest of the three-hour morning lesson. I tried my best to pay attention, but I didn't understand a thing. The lesson was about something called *fum,* which I suspected was math-related, but my translator had no idea what it meant. The teacher repeated the word about fifty times, and each time, the translator just beeped helplessly with an "unknown word" message.

Eventually the lesson ended, and all the kids headed for the door for what I figured must be lunch. As I started to follow them, the teacher approached me.

"How was the lesson for you, Lan Mifune?"

"Good! Thank you, sir!"

"Did you understand it?"

"Not really," I admitted. "But I'm sure I'll understand more as time goes on, sir."

"If you have questions, you may ask me."

"Thank you, sir! I will do that!" The class had emptied out by then, except for my soldier and Hooree. They were both waiting by the door.

"I am sorry you became upset during the questions," Yurinuri said. "In the future, I will try not to let that happen."

"Thank you, sir. I really appreciate it."

"Everyone agrees the human is violent," Yurinuri said, and my stomach dropped a little. But then he lowered his voice and continued, "But some people think you can evolve to be peaceful."

He seemed like he was trying not to let Hooree and the soldier hear him. I answered as quietly as I could. "I'm not violent, sir. I've never been violent. All the humans I know just want to live in peace."

Whatever you do, don't think about the food riot. I didn't want to start bawling again.

Yurinuri lowered his voice even further. "As I said, some people think this is possible. Some even think the human has positive things to offer our society. I am wondering—do you wish to explain more to the class about the human? Perhaps you can make a presentation that will help us better understand your species."

I nodded. "Yes, sir! I could definitely do that."

"Good! I am happy to help. If you have questions, you can ask me when class is not in session." Then he raised his voice to a normal level again. "Now—you should go to your midday nutrition! I am sorry to delay you and your guide."

"Thank you, sir!"

• • •

WHEN WE EXITED the classroom, the long hallway was mostly empty. I could hear the whine of hundreds of Zhuri voices coming from the far end. Hooree led me toward the sound as the soldier tagged along behind us.

"Please hurry," said Hooree. "You are making me late for my nutrition."

As I trotted down the hall, I tried to sort out what had just happened with my teacher. He definitely seemed like he wanted to help me. But he just as definitely didn't want Hooree and the soldier to hear him.

And what kind of presentation did he want me to make? A lecture? A video? About what, exactly? I had no idea.

We turned the corner at the end of the hall and entered an enormous room, open all the way to the skylight. It was buzzing with the noise of a couple thousand Zhuri kids, half of them in midair, all talking and flitting their wings. When I walked in, the ones closest to the door turned their heads to stare at me.

A second later, the fear smell hit my nose.

I looked around, trying to ignore the stares and the stink. Along the right-hand wall was a long, troughlike sink with a dozen faucets. The Zhuri stood in lines at each faucet, waiting to draw tall cups of their gross-tasting liquid food from them. The ones who'd already gotten their food sipped it through their long, needlelike mouths.

At the far end of the room was a big group of a few hundred Krik, all sitting together. Near the edge of the Krik group was a lone, gigantic Ororo. She was so big and blobby that from a distance I couldn't tell if she was standing or sitting.

Hooree pointed to the left-hand wall. "Your sister is over there," he said.

I could've found Ila just by following the stink of fear. She was sitting in the near corner, surrounded by a dozen empty stools, with only Iruu and her armed soldier for company.

Her face was pale, and she looked upset. When she saw me coming, she burst into tears.

"Hey, hey, hey." I moved quickly to an empty stool beside her and put my arm around her in a hug. She started to sob against my shoulder.

"It's okay. Really. Don't cry. It's okay." I felt like there'd already been more than enough bawling for one day.

"It's *not* okay," she said through her tears. "They *hate* us."

"Does she wish to eat food?" Iruu asked. "I have tried to help her, but she will not use her translator. And she keeps making body garbage with her eyes."

"This is not appropriate," Hooree whined. "It should not be making its body garbage in our lunchroom."

"It's not body garbage," I told him. "It's tears. That's just how humans show they're sad."

"It looks like body garbage to me. It is disgusting."

Why did they give me a guide who's such a jerk? I had to practically bite my tongue to stop myself from snapping at Hooree.

Iruu was much more kind. "Does she wish to eat food?" he asked again.

"Where's your lunch?" I asked Ila. Before we left for school that morning, we'd packed most of the leftover Ororo food into some old Chow containers.

"In the bag." Her bag was at her feet. I found her lunch inside it, along with her screen and earpiece. I handed her the lunch.

"Eat some of this. C'mon. It's delicious. You'll feel better."

"I have to go get my nutrition," Hooree announced. "Otherwise I will not have time to eat."

He flitted off. Iruu rubbed his wings together and looked conflicted—or at least I thought he did. It was tough for me to read the Zhuri's moods.

"You should go too, if you need food," I told Iruu. "We'll be fine."

He leaned in toward Ila. "Do not worry, Ila human," he said. "No one here will make disagreement on your face. We are peaceful."

Ila didn't say anything, but she managed a nod.

"Thanks, Iruu," I said. "We really appreciate it."

"You are welcome, Lan human. I will return as soon as I fetch my nutrition." He flitted off after Hooree, leaving us alone with our two guards. I managed to get Ila to start eating.

"We have to leave," she said miserably. "This is never going to work."

"It's just the first day."

"Do you smell how much they hate us?"

"That's just fear. Once they get to know us—"

"No, Lan—it's *anger*." She was right, sort of—underneath all the sour-milk stink was a faint but clear gasoline smell.

"The anger's not as bad. And that'll get better too. They just have to get to know us. My teacher's actually really nice."

"Mine isn't."

Her negativity made me clench my teeth in frustration. "Ila, we have to *try*." I bent over to fetch her screen and earpiece from her bag. "Here, why don't you turn your translator back on and—"

"*MRRRRRRUUMMMMMRRRRMMM.*"

I was still looking down at Ila's bag when the light suddenly dimmed, like something enormous had stepped in between me and the skylight.

Looking up, I found myself staring into a white-blue wall of velvety flesh. It rippled with leftover movement, like a pond after a rock had been thrown into it.

I heard Ila gasp in fear as I looked up into the dark, wet eyes of the only Ororo in the room. From a distance, those eyes had looked sleepy. But at such close range, they were fierce.

"*MMMRRRUUUUMMMMMMM,*" it said again, its voice so deep that I could feel its rumble through the floor. My translator beeped its "unknown language" warning.

Ila whimpered.

"Hello," I said to the Ororo, trying to stay calm. "I'm sorry, but my translator can't understand you."

"*MRRRMMMM.*" Its tree trunk–thick arm rose from its side, and it held out its giant fleshy hand.

Did it want to shake my hand? Was that a thing the Ororo did? Or if I tried to shake it, would it think I was attacking and freak out?

"My name is Lan," I said, because I didn't know what else to say. I hoped it could understand the Zhuri translation coming out of my speaker clip.

"*MRRRMMM!*" It jiggled its open hand, making more ripples spread across its body.

"*GRZZZRRKK!*" The sudden noise made me jump in fright.

There was a razor-toothed Krik standing next to the Ororo, practically underneath its arm.

Had that Krik been standing there the whole time?

"GZZZRRK!" The Krik was growling at me through its double row of teeth.

"Hello," I said in a shaky voice. "My name is Lan."

"ZZZRRKK!" The Krik pointed to Ila's screen, which I was still holding. I realized that was why the Ororo had been holding its hand out.

I raised the screen to show the Ororo, keeping a tight grip with both hands. "This is for communicating. It translates for us, so we can speak Zhuri. And also understand it. Can you understand what I'm saying?"

"MRRRRMMM." The Ororo shook its giant hand again.

"GZZRRK!" The Krik pointed to the screen, then to the Ororo's hand.

"This one belongs to my sister," I said. "And this is my sister! Her name is Ila."

"Hello," said Ila in a terrified whisper.

"MRRRMMMM." The Ororo brought its hand down on the screen. It was warm, squishy, and so big that it covered not just the whole screen, but almost all of my hands too.

The Ororo tightened its grip. My heart was hammering against my chest.

I looked around for our guards. They were sitting a few feet away, casually sucking down their lunch and not making any move to get involved.

"Please help!" Ila cried to them. She didn't have her translator on, but it was obvious what she was saying.

The soldiers kept eating, their weapons lying across their laps.

"Can you talk to them for us?" I begged the soldiers.

They just stared at me in response. "It is not our job to make translation," one of them said.

We were on our own. The Ororo's grip was getting tighter.

"I'm sorry," I told it, "but I can't—"

"*YEEEEHHEEEEEE!*"

"GET AWAY FROM THE HUMANS!"

It was Hooree, back from fetching his liquid lunch. At his shriek, the Ororo relaxed its grip enough that I managed to snatch Ila's screen back. I hugged it against my chest as all three of them—Hooree, the Ororo, and its little Krik sidekick—had a brief but loud argument.

"Leave them alone! You are not wanted here!"

"*MRRMMMRR.*"

"*GZZZRRKK!*"

"No! I am its guide! Get away from here, criminal!"

"*MRRRMM.*"

"*ZZRKZZRRK!*"

The Ororo gave up, turning and lumbering away. The Krik let out a final growl, then followed its partner as Iruu returned.

"What happened?" he asked.

"Marf the criminal tried to steal the human's translator screen," said Hooree.

I watched the Ororo head back to the Krik section of the cafeteria. As big as it was, it somehow managed to cross the floor so fast that its little green sidekick had to work its short legs double time to keep up.

"The Ororo's a criminal?" I asked.

"She is a terrible criminal," said Hooree. "Everyone agrees she should be expelled from our school. But she is too smart for the learning specialists to catch her."

"Is that Krik a criminal too?"

"He probably is," said Iruu. "Otherwise it does not make sense that they are friends."

"Why not?" I asked.

"Because Ororo would never spend time with Krik. The Krik like to eat them."

I thought back to all the food-related questions the Krik in my class had asked. "Would Krik eat humans?"

"Maybe," said Iruu.

"If you wriggled a lot while they ate you, they would definitely like that," Hooree added.

Ila clutched my hand in hers. "We can't stay on this planet," she whispered.

I gave her hand a squeeze. "Don't worry," I told her. "We're going to be okay."

But I didn't really believe it.

10

INVASION OF
THE SCREEN SNATCHERS

I SOMEHOW MADE it through the rest of the day without getting eaten, attacked, or so upset that I burst into tears. When school ended, Hooree and I met Iruu and Ila in the lobby, and they walked us with our guards to an unmanned pod in front of the entrance. There was still a cluster of about fifty Zhuri protestors on the far side of the fence, and they chanted "HUMANS GO HOME!" until we flew out of hearing range.

Ila and I both shut our translators off. The two guards were still with us, but we'd given up even trying to talk to them.

"For a first day, it could've been worse," I said.

My sister didn't say anything. She just lay down across one of the benches that lined the pod walls, curled up in a ball, and shut her eyes.

I checked my screen. There was a message from Naya.

How's it going? Are you a good doggie? Send me video!

Mom had warned us that since people up on the ship were desperate and scared, we should only send messages that were hopeful. I typed in a short reply:

It's great! First day of school just ended, and nobody's eaten me yet! Will send vid soon.

That was about as hopeful as I could manage. Then I messaged Mom and Dad on their screens:

School over. Heading home. How are you guys doing?

Neither of them answered, so I stared out the window for a while and tried to think of a good video message to record for Naya. The two I'd sent so far were so bland and chirpy—*Look at this beautiful red grass and green sky! The air smells so good! We're having some government officials over for dinner! Ruff, ruff!*—that I was worried if I didn't send her something funny, she'd think I was either brainwashed or lying.

The problem was that I couldn't figure out how to be funny and hopeful at the same time.

I was still racking my brain about it when I saw the protestors. There were dozens of them outside the fence at the edge of our subdivision. When our pod passed overhead, they flitted into the air and started their usual "HUMANS GO HOME!" chant. The noise of the fence crossing woke Ila, and she moaned when she heard the chant.

Inside the house with the door closed, we could still hear them in the distance. Ila shuffled off to her room. "I'm going to bed."

"It's the middle of the afternoon! You want to play a game? Watch some *Birdleys*?"

Instead of answering, she shut the door. When I went in after her, she was already lying in bed.

"Ila, c'mon. Don't go to your dark place."

"Leave me alone!"

I gave up and left her to sulk, closing the bedroom door behind me. Then I went to the kitchen in search of Ororo food, but there was nothing except Chow. Mom and Dad must've taken the last of the leftovers with them for their lunches.

I messaged them again, then flopped down on the Ororo-sized couch. After our beds, the couch was the best piece of furniture in the house. It wasn't low to the floor like the beds, so you practically had to climb onto it. Once you did, the big plush cushions swallowed you up and gently massaged you. It was like floating in a warm pond filled with very friendly, slightly grabby fish.

I was starting to doze off when I heard the boom of a pod crossing the fence. I got up and looked out the window, expecting to see Mom and Dad coming home in one of the usual pill-shaped beige pods.

But the pod coming in for a landing was a whole other thing: gleaming silver chrome, dagger-shaped and sleek, with little winglike flourishes that reminded me of the tail fins on antique cars back on Earth. It looked twice as fast and ten times as expensive as the usual pods.

After it touched down in front of our house, its door hovered open dramatically, and an Ororo and a Krik emerged. At the sight of them, I sucked in my breath. They looked like the same pair who'd tried to steal Ila's screen at lunch.

For a second I thought about pretending nobody was home. But Hooree had said they were criminals, and I figured my odds were better if I met them at the door, where there were two armed guards. I doubted the guards would actually help me, but I was hoping they'd at least make the criminals think twice.

As the visitors approached, I threw the door open and stood in the middle of the doorway, trying not to look as scared as I felt.

"MRRRRMMMMMRRRMM."

"GZZZZZRRRK!"

"Sirs," I asked the guards, "can you please tell me what they're saying?"

"They say they are here to fix your translator," one of them explained.

"Did someone *ask* them to fix my translator?"

"They must have gotten approval from the government," the second one told me. "Otherwise their pod would have crashed when it crossed the fence."

"Can you ask who sent them here?"

"It is not our job to translate for you," said the first guard.

"MRRRMMMMM." The Ororo barreled right at me. I had to step back and let her in, or I would've gotten flattened.

The Krik followed her inside and shut the door. At that point, the guards couldn't hear me anymore unless I screamed. And even then, they might not help.

"MRRMMMMM." The Ororo held out her giant hand like she'd done in the cafeteria, beckoning for me to give her my screen.

"I need this to communicate," I told her. "It's precious. If I don't have it, I can't understand the Zhuri."

"MRRRMMMMM."

"GZZZRK!"

"There are engineers up on the human ship," I said. "They're working to fix the translator so it can understand you. They think in a couple of weeks it'll be ready. Maybe you could come back then?"

The Ororo clamped her hand down on mine. This time she wasn't going to take no for an answer. And between her giant size and the Krik's sharp teeth, putting up a fight seemed hopeless.

I gave up and let her have the screen. "Please be careful with it," I begged as she flipped it over in her hand, examining it closely with her dark liquid eyes.

The Krik peeked over the side of the Ororo's giant arm to stare at the screen too. His mouth hung open a little, the razor-sharp teeth glistening with spit.

"MRRMMM." The Ororo walked over to the dining table and put down my screen. Ila had left her own screen on the table, and when I saw it lying there, I worried the Ororo would snatch it too.

Instead she pushed it aside. Then she sat down on one of the wide, low chairs.

The Krik hopped up onto the chair next to her. He was carrying a small satchel, and when he opened it, I got a glimpse of all sorts of complicated-looking tech inside.

He pulled out two skeletal tools that looked like robotic hands and handed them to the Ororo. She flipped my screen over so its back was facing up, and in movements so quick they were practically a blur, she used the tools to pull off the back of the screen. Long, needlelike extensions telescoped out from the tips of the mechanical fingers, and she plunged them into the screen's hardware.

"Please don't do that!" I practically screamed as a sudden crackle of static burst through my earpiece.

She ignored me, digging into the screen's guts with the needle ends of both robotic hands. The static in my ear was so loud that I had to pull the earpiece out. I wondered if I should go back to the guards outside and ask them to call the police for me. But I suspected the guards actually *were* the police—and if so, they weren't interested in taking my side.

I considered calling out for Ila, but the fact that she hadn't come out already made me think she must be either asleep or hiding. Either way, she wouldn't be much help.

After a minute of rooting around, the Ororo turned the screen so the front was facing her. Numbers and letters of human code cascaded down the display. She watched them closely as she kept digging into the back with the needles.

I was trying to remember where Mom and Dad had put the backup screens they'd brought with us when I heard muffled voices coming from the earpiece in my hand. I stuck it back in my ear.

> *"This is my voice. . . ."*
> **"THIS IS MY VOICE. . . ."**
> *"Thees ees my voeeece. . . ."*
> **"Thizzz muh voice. . . ."**

The Ororo seemed to be testing out my translator's different voice signatures. She flipped on the screen's external speaker and cycled through a few dozen of them, occasionally mumbling questions for the Krik, who answered them with his usual snappish growls.

Then, suddenly—

"GZZZRKKK."

"Yes! I want that one." A grumpy old comedian's voice came through my earpiece.

"MRRMMMM."

"Very well. And this will be mine." It was the low-pitched, sexy-sounding rasp of a famous actress.

The Ororo replaced the back of my screen, returned the tools to the Krik, and handed the screen to me.

"Here you are," she said through my translator. "Now it works. I told you there was nothing to fear. Although of course you couldn't understand what I was saying. My name is Marf. And this is Ezger."

"Hello," I said. "My name is Lan." I tried not to sound as confused as I felt. She'd barged into my house without asking and had practically robbed me. But she sounded friendly—or at least her voice signature did.

"What kind of food do you have?" Ezger asked. He hopped off the chair and headed for our kitchen.

"Just some human stuff," I told him. "It's not very good."

He jumped up on the kitchen's countertop and started to rummage through the upper drawers.

"Please don't do that!"

He ignored me. I didn't want to get in a fight with somebody who looked capable of swallowing my head, so I turned my attention back to Marf the Ororo.

"How did you fix the translator so fast?" I asked her. "The human engineers on our ship said it'd take weeks."

"Do you understand mathematics?"

"Kind of."

The corners of Marf's mouth turned up in what seemed like a smile. "The average Ororo is seven thousand times as smart as the average human. Does that answer your question?"

"Pretty much."

A loud crash came from the kitchen. Ezger had accidentally pulled a drawer off its runner.

"The food's in the third drawer down on the right," I said. "Yes, that one." He pulled out a container of Chow.

"I apologize for Ezger's manners," said Marf. "For a Krik, he is very polite. But that is not saying much."

"Who sent you here?" I asked.

"No one," said Marf. "That was a lie I told the guards so they would not know I overrode the security features on the fence. But don't worry—you are safe from the protestors. Only the Ororo are clever enough to override a fence, and none of them would bother to come here except me."

I had so many questions that I almost didn't know where to start. "So . . . why did you come here? Just for the food?"

Ezger sniffed the Chow and made a face. "That would have been a big mistake," he growled. "This food looks terrible!"

"We came to convert you to our religion," Marf told me.

"Really?"

"Oh yes!" Marf's mouth turned up even further. This time I

was sure it was a smile. "Its rituals are very painful. As part of the initiation, Ezger will have to chew off one of your arms. But you will find great spiritual meaning in your suffering."

A little surge of fear shot straight to my brain. "I'm so sorry," I said. "But I already have a religion."

"That is fine," said Marf. "I was only making a joke. Do humans have jokes?"

"Yes! Do you?"

"Marf does," said Ezger. "But her jokes are never funny."

"Only because you have no sense of humor, Ezger," Marf told him. Ezger shrugged and went back to examining our Chow with a look of disgust.

"I thought people on Choom didn't like jokes," I said.

Marf shook her enormous head. "Oh no. The Zhuri *government* doesn't like jokes. But that is very different. Tell me a human joke."

"This food is a human joke!" Ezger barked. He held up the Chow to show Marf. "It looks like feces!"

"It tastes like it too," I admitted.

"Ah!" Marf's big, dark eyes grew even bigger, and her smile widened as she put her giant, warm hand on my back. "Now, *that* is a joke." She turned to Ezger, who was shoving the Chow back in its drawer without closing the container. "You see, Ezger? I am glad we came. I told you the human would be entertaining."

"So you're here to . . . be entertained?"

"That was my hope. Choom desperately needs entertainment. You have no idea how boring this planet is."

"This kitchen is certainly boring," Ezger grumbled, sticking his head into an empty cabinet. "Don't you have any food that moves?"

"No. Sorry about that."

He pulled his head back out and shook it in disappointment. "Then there is no point in staying. Marf, can we leave now?"

"We only just got here!" said Marf. "I have not even asked to borrow the human's screen yet." Ila's screen was still lying on the dining table. Marf picked it up with her massive hand. "Is this an extra one? May I take it with me?"

"I'm sorry. That belongs to my sister."

"I will give it back to her at school tomorrow morning. I just want to study it."

"Marf will definitely return it," Ezger told me. "Will you please loan it to her so we can leave?"

"Ezger, you are being *very* rude," Marf scolded him. Then she picked up Ila's screen. "So may I borrow this?"

"I'm so sorry," I said, "but I can't let you. My sister needs it to communicate."

Marf reluctantly set it back down. "I told you I will give it back. Do you not trust me?"

"I do!" I said quickly. "I just, um . . ."

The truth was, I didn't. Marf could tell I was lying.

"It's because that Hooree person told you I'm a criminal, isn't it?"

"No!" I yelped. "I mean . . . he did say that. But I didn't believe it."

"Good. Because it is not true at all."

"Yes, it is!" barked Ezger. "You are *definitely* a criminal! You break laws all the time!"

"I only break silly laws," said Marf. "Not important ones." She turned back to me. "I do wish you would trust me. After all, I trusted you enough to come here even though my television says you are a violent murderer."

"It does?"

"Yes. But don't take it personally. According to the television, *all* humans are violent murderers."

Ugh. "Do a lot of people watch television?"

"Of course! Everyone does."

"How can I watch it? I'd like to know what they're saying about humans. But I haven't even seen a television on this planet."

"Are you stupid?" Ezger asked me. "There is one on your wall."

He marched over to the couch. On the floor in front of it was a hex-shaped tile in a slightly different shade of beige from the rest of the tiles.

"Just press this three times." He tapped on the mismatched tile with his foot—one, two, three—and a section of floor in front of the couch opened like a trapdoor. A meter-long control panel rose up from the open floor while a giant screen appeared on the wall opposite the couch.

On the screen, a Zhuri stood in front of a three-dimensional model of the planet, pointing to the bottom of it.

"Storms at the southern pole will weaken overnight . . . ," he was saying.

"There are four channels," Marf explained. "This one is weather. There is also the news channel, the 'clearing the air' channel, and the Krik channel."

"The Krik channel is the best," said Ezger. "It is all cooking shows."

Marf trundled over to the control panel and showed me how it worked. "This button changes the channel, this is the volume, this pauses and rewinds, and this turns the unit off."

I watched the Zhuri on the screen give his planetary weather report. "This is unbelievable. We've been living here for days, and we had no idea there was a TV in the wall."

"I suppose you will want to watch it now," said Marf, "so we will leave you alone."

"Finally!" grumbled Ezger, heading for the door.

"You don't have to leave!" I said. "I'd much rather talk to you than watch TV."

"Don't worry," said Marf, waddling after the Krik. "We can talk again tomorrow during the midday nutrition. It was very nice to meet you, Lan human."

"Just Lan," I said. "Please come back anytime!"

"Not if you don't get better food, we won't," growled Ezger.

"Oh! Wait!" As Ezger held the door open, Marf turned to look back at me. "Speaking of food," I said, "do you know how we can get more of the Ororo food? We love it, but we ran out."

"I can get you as much as you want," Marf told me. "For a price. How about a ten-day supply for eight hundred *rhee*?"

"I'm sorry—what are rhee?"

Ezger snorted. "'What are rhee?' Ridiculous. I'll be in the pod." He disappeared out the door.

"Don't touch the flight controls!" Marf called after him. Then she sighed. "Ezger is a very bad pilot. But he *thinks* he is a very good one. It is a dangerous combination. Where were we? Oh yes—rhee! Rhee is money."

"Oh." That took the air out of my sails. "I'm sorry. I don't have any money."

"Then I am sorry too," said Marf, "because I can't give you food without payment. I am a businessperson. It was bad enough that I fixed your translator for free. Enjoy the television! Goodbye."

Just like that, she was gone. Seconds later, I heard the thunder-clap of their pod crossing the fence and wondered how she'd been able to override its security code.

There were a lot of things I wondered about her and Ezger. Their whole visit had been so strange and sudden that I felt like I was in a state of mild shock.

Then I sat down on the couch and turned my attention to the TV.

I was about to get a whole lot more shocked.

NEWS, WEATHER, AND HATE

THE FIRST THING I saw when I switched past the weather must've been the "clearing the air" channel. It was a plain beige background, broadcasting a low *yeeeeehheeee* white-noise whine that I guessed was soothing to the Zhuri.

The next one was the Krik channel. It was a close-up of one of the wriggling yeero vegetables. An unseen Krik's hand cut into it with a knife as he snarled instructions:

"We're going to cut right across the grain here, then shove our spices in real deep for a flavor explosion. KA-BLAM! But don't cook it for too long, or it'll lose its wriggle. . . ."

Finally I got to the news channel. At first it was broadcasting video of an enormous spaceship orbiting some kind of gas-giant planet while an announcer explained the situation:

"Due to continued atmospheric disturbances on Zemrock Six, *yeeneeree* gas capture operations were suspended for the ninth consecutive day. The interruption has led to an increase in yeeneeree raw-material prices of almost forty percent. . . ."

After that there was a story about pod manufacturing that

dragged on forever and was basically impossible to understand. I was about to change the channel back to the Krik cooking show when the segment ended, and they started talking about us.

It began with a clip of Ila and me arriving at school that morning.

"Under an agreement made many years ago, the four human animals entered schools and workplaces for the first time today. . . ."

"Ila!" I yelled, loud enough to wake my sister. "Come see this!"

I watched us greet Hooree, Iruu, and the principal at the school's front door while our guards stood watch behind us. There was no sound, so you couldn't tell from the clip that there were screaming protestors just a few yards away.

"The two younger humans enrolled at the Iseeyii Interspecies Academy. While no acts of violence were reported, everyone agrees the humans are impossible to educate."

The image switched to an interview with a Zhuri student. At first I didn't recognize him. But then I heard the little-old-lady voice signature come through my translator, and I realized it was Hooree.

"The human is very primitive," he told a news reporter. "The learning specialist explains concepts, and it understands nothing."

"What?" As big a jerk as Hooree had been, I couldn't believe he'd insult me like that on television.

Ila appeared at her bedroom door, squinting and scowling like I'd just woken her up. "Was somebody here? And what are you yelling—" Then she saw the TV. "Ohmygosh! Where did that come from?"

"Shhhhh! Just watch!"

The video switched to a shot of Mom walking into a large building, trailed by two armed guards.

"Due to their low mental ability, the adult humans were assigned jobs in the waste-removal and mortuary sectors. This afternoon, security forces were called to Waste Facility Seven Six Seven, where one of the humans attacked a Zhuri supervisor."

The image switched to some kind of industrial site. Against a backdrop of building-sized machinery, half a dozen Zhuri with weapons led Dad away as a group of Krik looked on.

Dad's hands were stuck inside some kind of toaster oven–sized handcuffs, and the whole left side of his face was bright red and badly swollen.

Ila and I both screamed at the sight of his injury.

"AAAIIIEEEE!"

"OHMYGOSH! OHMYGOSH!"

The video cut away from Dad to show a wasteland of churned-up ground and barbed wire. It looked like an old Earth film of a World War I battlefield.

"Everyone agrees such violence was predictable . . . ," said the announcer.

"WHAT HAPPENED TO DAD?"

"I don't know!"

On the screen, men with guns emerged from trenches to shoot at each other, and I suddenly realized it actually *was* an old Earth film of World War I.

"Humans are an aggressive and emotional species, whose violence is so extreme that they destroyed their home planet...."

"Ohmygosh ...," Ila whispered in horror as the World War I footage gave way to a more modern war, with fighter planes dropping bombs on a jungle village ... then a firing squad of soldiers, shooting unarmed civilians ... then a nuclear bomb, exploding over a city....

"As these images from the ruined human planet show, they are unfit to live among the civilized people of Choom. While everyone agrees the Unified Government was correct to honor its promise to offer the human reproductive unit refuge on a trial basis ..."

Two martial-arts fighters squared off in a ring, beating each other senseless.... Then a man in a clown suit slashed a woman with a kitchen knife....

"That's a HORROR MOVIE!" I yelled. "It's not even real!"

"Shhh!"

"... everyone also agrees the experiment in human resettlement will fail, and the hundreds of humans currently in orbit above Choom will not be allowed to land and further disrupt our peace. Stay tuned for more updates on the human threat."

The story ended, and the video switched to a shot of dozens of Zhuri flitting through the air and shrieking as they passed a suswut disc back and forth.

"In last night's regional suswut semifinal, Team Eight Four defeated Team Eight One by a score of three thousand six hundred and twelve to ...."

"What did they do to Dad?" I hit the pause button and started to rewind back to the footage of Dad's injury.

"Have you messaged him?" Ila went back to the dining table to get her screen.

"Twice. Him and Mom both. They haven't answered." I found the segment of Dad getting led away by guards and replayed it. The second time around, the injury to his face looked even worse. Watching it made me sick to my stomach.

"Where's my screen?" Ila said from behind me.

"It's on the table."

"No, it isn't."

"It's right there—" I turned around to point at the spot on the table where Marf had left Ila's screen.

It wasn't there anymore.

"Oh no . . ."

"What?"

"Marf stole it."

"What?"

We spent the next half hour yelling at each other, rewatching the horrifying news clips on Zhuri TV, and frantically messaging Mom and Dad with a growing sense of panic that didn't let up until we finally got a reply from Mom:

> Your father is ok sorry we couldn't respond
> sooner home ASAP love mom

They came home twenty minutes later. Leeni was with them. Dad's face was bandaged, and so was the upper half of his left side. Even bandaged up, he looked much worse than he had on the TV.

"Ish okay," he slurred through his swollen mouth. "Doeshn't even hurt zhaht mush."

I could tell he was lying.

"The venom's effect should decrease over time," said Leeni. "Hopefully, in the morning, you will have recovered."

"What happened?"

"Your father got assigned to a Krik garbage crew," Mom explained. "And their Zhuri supervisor doesn't like humans."

"The supervisor will be reassigned," Leeni told us. "This will not happen again."

"On the TV it looked like Dad got arrested," I said.

Mom nodded. "He did. The supervisor claimed Dad tried to attack him. But the Krik who were there stuck up for Dad." She looked over at the TV. "Can I watch the news report?"

"I do not think this is a good idea," said Leeni. "The television will only make you emotional."

Mom ignored Leeni's advice. We all sat on the couch and watched the broadcast again. To be fair, Leeni was right—it was the fourth or fifth time I'd seen it, and every time I did, the report made me more upset and angry.

"That last clip isn't even real!" I told Leeni when it was over. "It was from a movie!"

"What is a movie?" Leeni asked me.

"It's entertainment. A made-up story. For fun. That clip of the woman getting killed was totally fake! She was an actor—she didn't even get hurt in real life!"

Leeni fixed his big compound eyes on me. "Humans find it entertaining to watch each other die in horrible ways? That is fun for you?"

When he put it that way, I did have to admit it sounded a little questionable.

"Leeni," Mom said in her most calm, gentle, *I'm begging you to help us* voice, "this news report does not tell the full truth about humans. It's not even the full truth of what happened today. Kalil was innocent—the supervisor attacked *him*. And outside my workplace, hundreds of Zhuri protestors screamed horrible things and tried to spit venom at me as I came and went. Why does your television not show any of this?"

"The Executive Division believes it is not responsible to show disagreement by Zhuri on television," Leeni said. "It causes emotion."

Hearing that, Ila blew up. "What the—"

"Ila, *please*." Mom reached out a hand to settle her down.

Even though I kept my mouth shut, I was every bit as upset as my sister. It wasn't that I thought humans weren't violent at all. We had a bad side—I'd seen it myself during those last hours on Earth and even after that, when the food riot happened on Mars. But we weren't all bad. We had a good side too. And it was infuriating to get called violent and primitive by a bunch of people who'd attacked us in a mob the second we set foot on their planet, then tried to pretend *they* were the peaceful ones.

Mom was mad too. But she kept her voice low and steady. "Leeni, if I saw these images and knew nothing else about humans, I would fear us too. Do you see how unfair this is? How the television is creating this fear and hatred?"

Leeni rubbed his wings together awkwardly. "I agree the television does not seem to show a complete picture of the human."

"How can we change this? Can we appear on this program and explain ourselves?"

"I am sorry," Leeni said. "The Executive Division controls the television news."

"Can we ask someone in the Executive Division about doing an interview?"

"The Immigration Division has made this request several times. The answer was no."

"Isn't there some way we can change their minds?"

"I am sorry," Leeni repeated. "The Immigration Division has discussed this at great length with the Executive Division. Their choices about how to portray the human on television will not change. But . . ."

He stopped talking, pressing his wings together so hard that I could hear them scratch against each other.

"But what?" Mom asked.

Instead of answering, Leeni flitted to the door. "I am sorry— I must leave now." He turned to look back at Dad. "I hope your injury heals quickly, Kalil. And I wish you all a peaceful evening."

Then he left, briefly letting in the "HUMANS GO HOME!" whine of the distant protestors before the door shut behind him.

"What do you make of that 'but'?" Mom asked us.

Ila was sitting next to Dad, her hand on his back. She snorted. "What does it matter? Look what they did to Dad!"

"Ish not sho bahd," he slurred.

"Yes, it is!" Ila insisted. "Listen to the TV: 'Everyone agrees' they're going to kick us out of here! They *hate* us!"

Mom shook her head. "Not all of them. When they say 'everyone agrees,' it's not true. They *don't* all agree. They're just afraid to disagree out loud. I had a Zhuri coworker today who was, like . . ." Mom deepened her voice, imitating a Zhuri translation.

" 'Everyone agrees the human cannot stay!' But when the others weren't around, he was like"—she lowered her voice to a half whisper—" 'but some people think they can.' "

"My teacher's like that," I said. "He's really nice to me—but he's quiet about it, like he doesn't want people to hear him. And he said the same thing today: 'Some people think humans can be peaceful.' "

"The question is," Mom asked, "how many people think that?"

Ila shook her head. "No. The question is, why does it matter what a couple of people are whispering to us when hundreds of them scream 'Humans go home!' every time we leave the house?"

"It matters," Mom said in a firm voice, "because we have to start somewhere. We can make this work. I know we can."

MOM'S CONFIDENCE MADE me feel a lot better than Ila's doom and gloom. It had been a long, sometimes horrible day, and it took me forever to fall asleep that night. But every time one of the bad moments raced across my mind—the screaming protestors, the awful question-and-answer session in class, Dad's injury, the TV news—I forced myself to be positive like Mom, and to think about one of the good things instead. The principal's welcome, my teacher's quiet encouragement, Iruu's kindness when Ila was freaking out, the weird but mostly friendly visit from Marf and Ezger . . . I didn't know what they all added up to, but it had to be something.

Mom was right: it was a start. I just had to stay as positive as she was.

I lay awake so long that eventually I had to get up and pee. When I got to the bathroom, the door was locked, and I could hear muffled sobbing on the other side.

I knocked hard on the door. I was about to open my mouth and yell, *Ila! Go bawl in your own room!*

But then a voice answered my knock, and it wasn't Ila's.

"Just a minute!" I heard Mom say, sounding ragged and embarrassed.

I stood there in the hallway for a moment, too stunned to answer. Then I scooted back to bed as fast as I could. A minute later, I heard my door open softly.

"Lan . . . ?" Mom whispered.

I pretended I was asleep, and she tiptoed away. I knew she'd come to try to make me feel better, but I didn't want to hear it. I just wanted to forget the sound of her sobs coming through the door.

The trouble was, I couldn't.

12

THE MYSTERIOUS SMELL
OF DOUGHNUTS

THE NEXT MORNING, the swelling from Dad's venom attack hadn't gotten better. He couldn't eat or open his left eye, so he stayed home from work.

Ila stayed with him. "Somebody has to take care of Dad," she said, lying curled up on the couch as she watched a Krik cooking show.

"How are you going to take care of him when you're lying on the couch?" I asked.

"I'll get up in a minute."

It seemed unlikely, but I didn't want to make Mom and Dad upset by fighting with my sister. So I packed some Chow for lunch and went outside with Mom to wait for our pods.

"Get my screen back from that Ororo!" Ila snarled at me as we left.

"I'll try!" Even though we had two spare screens, Ila was furious with me for letting Marf steal hers, because it had twenty *Birdleys* episodes and all her old *Pop Singer* performances on it. There were copies of them in the server library up on the transport, but the download speeds to Choom were lousy, and being separated from those *Pop Singer* clips of the greatest moments of her old life was making my sister even more crabby and difficult than usual. It made me suspect she was probably still watching them whenever she was alone, which was really irritating. Sulking over the past wasn't going to help us win over the Zhuri, and we needed all the help we could get.

A few dozen protestors were outside the fence at the far end of the subdivision. When they saw Mom and me walk onto the lawn, they started their "HUMANS GO HOME!" chant.

"Would you rather go back inside to wait?" Mom asked.

"It's fine," I said. "There aren't enough of them to bother me. Or maybe I'm just getting used to it."

Mom gave me a little hug and a kiss on the cheek. "Thanks for going to school today. I know it's not easy doing it alone. And, hey, I'm sorry about—"

"So what's your job like?" I blurted out. I knew by the sound of her voice that she was about to bring up the bathroom incident, and I didn't want to go there.

"Hmm? Oh. It's pretty unpleasant. They've got me working in a morgue."

"Is that as bad as it sounds?"

Mom let out a dry chuckle. "It might be worse. But I'm not complaining." She looked up at the green sky. "There's a thousand humans up there, counting on us to help them get off that ship. That's what really matters right now."

"I owe Naya a video," I said.

"You can talk to her live when they're on this side of the planet. Just make sure you stay positive."

"I know. That's why I don't want to talk to her live."

"Hey, Lan: I want to explain—"

"It's okay, Mom. We don't have to talk about it."

"We do, though. I'm sorry about last night. I was having a . . . less-than-brave moment. And I'm sure it was scary for you to hear that. But do you remember what I said to you when we got on the shuttle to come here?"

" 'Buckle your seat belt'?"

"Probably that too . . . But I told you it's okay to be scared. And we can be scared and brave at the same time. That's true for *all* of us. This is a frightening situation. If we weren't afraid, we'd be doing it wrong. And sometimes that fear seems overwhelming, even to me. But it's not. *We can do this.* We just need courage. And courage doesn't mean we ignore our fear. It just means we move through it. Okay?"

"I am not afraid," I said. " 'Everyone agrees' I am not afraid at all, Mom human."

She smirked. " 'Some people think' you *are* afraid, Lan human."

" 'Everyone agrees' that is not true. I am *not* making a fear smell. I just have bad gas."

She hugged me tight. "I love you, kid."

"I love you too. Quit hogging the bathroom at night."

THE PODS SHOWED up, and I said goodbye to Mom. When I got on mine, there were two guards inside.

"Good morning, sirs." I gave them a halfhearted smile. It was getting harder to stay golden-retriever friendly all the time.

"Where is the other human?"

"She's not coming to school today."

After they found out only one human needed guarding, they spent the rest of the pod trip arguing about which one of them should get the rest of the day off. It was pretty amusing to listen to—since there were only two of them, nobody could play the "everyone agrees" card, so the argument went on forever.

HOOREE AND IRUU met me just inside the school lobby. When Iruu found out Ila wasn't coming, he looked disappointed. Hooree was just offended.

"This is very rude of your sibling," he said. "Attending school is a great honor. She insults us by staying home."

"Speaking of insults . . ." My voice trembled a little with nerves, but I'd already decided I had to call him out on his interview. "I saw you call me primitive on the TV yesterday."

"That is not an insult," he told me. "It is the truth."

My heart thumped faster. "I don't think I'm primitive. I think I'm just new here."

"If you can't even understand fum, you are definitely primitive."

Iruu rubbed his wings together like he had a bad itch. "Everyone agrees we should get along," he whined.

I felt my face turn hot. No matter how bad Hooree was, fighting with one of the only Zhuri who was willing to talk to me was probably a stupid move. "I agree!" I said, trying to smile. "I am sorry if I offended you, Hooree."

He ignored the apology. "Do not make me late to class," he said. Then he turned and flitted off.

"Have a nice day, Iruu!" I yelled over my shoulder as I ran to catch up with my jerk of an escort. The guard who'd lost the argument in the pod followed me down the hallway. So did the stink of fear. It wasn't as bad as it had been on the first day, but it seemed like every Zhuri kid I passed let off at least a little of it.

Hooree moved so quickly that I almost lost sight of him in the crowd. I picked up my pace to a trot, and when he ducked into our classroom, I followed him through the door a little too fast and wound up bumping into him.

"Do not touch me!" he shrieked, so loudly that the whole classroom turned to stare at us.

"I am so sorry!"

I backed away as fast as I could, tripped over an empty stool, and wound up crashing to the floor in a fall that I made even uglier by flailing my arms as I went down.

Zhuri voices erupted all around me.

"Did you see it?"

"Did you see the human fall?"

Before I could even stand up, a smell hit my nose—the same sugary, baked-doughnut scent that I'd caught a whiff of from Iruu when I'd imitated a Nug before the dinner party.

"Are you injured, Lan human?" Yurinuri flitted over to stare down at me with what must've been concern.

"I am fine!" I scrambled to my feet and managed a smile. "I am sorry if I caused a problem!"

"Accidents are never a problem," said Yurinuri. Then he

swiveled his head back and forth to take in the whole class. "Clear the air, children," he said. "Everyone agrees smell is not polite."

A moment later, I was in my seat, and the doughnut smell was gone, leaving me to wonder what the heck it meant.

It seemed like they'd been laughing at me. Was that possible? Did the Zhuri laugh? Hooree and Leeni had both said people should not make jokes. But Iruu had said that some people thought it was okay. And Marf had said that only the Zhuri *government* didn't like jokes. Maybe that meant some of the Zhuri *did* like jokes?

And that doughnut smell meant they were laughing?

The lesson started, and I had to quit wondering about the smell, because I was too busy trying to figure out what Yurinuri was trying to teach us. It had something to do with *urm,* which he said should be easy to understand, because it was "the companion of fum."

Since I had no idea what fum was, this didn't really help.

After a while, Yurinuri started writing what must've been equations on the wall screen, then asking kids to come up and solve them using a laser marker. It was entertaining to watch, because all the Zhuri kids acted the same way. They'd lope up to the front of the class with their bendy-legged, absurd-looking walk, then shake their heads in a little wriggle before they started to scratch out an answer.

If they got the answer right, Yurinuri congratulated them. As they bounced back to their stools, their wings would twitch, and they'd flit up a few inches off the floor in what I guessed was either pride or happiness. But when they got the answer wrong, Yurinuri would thank them for trying, and they'd hang their heads as they silly-walked back to their seats.

Watching the Zhuri kids, I felt a weird urge to imitate them. But I wasn't sure anybody would get the joke. And even if they did, I wasn't sure if they'd appreciate it. Would any of them laugh? Or would they just get offended?

I didn't know. There was so much I didn't know.

WHEN YURINURI DISMISSED us for lunch, I tagged after Hooree to ask him about the smell.

"When I fell down in class, people made a smell—"

"They should not have made smell. It was very rude of them."

"But what was it?"

"I told you. It was rude!"

"I know. But I mean, what kind of emotion were they making?"

"The only thing more rude than making smell," Hooree said in an even higher-pitched whine than usual, "is *talking* about smell."

As we approached the lunchroom, I started to worry about what would happen when I saw Marf. She'd stolen Ila's screen, and I needed to get it back. But what if she denied stealing it? What if I confronted her and she attacked me? She didn't seem violent, but even her friend Ezger said she was a criminal. What if she sat on me? Or told Ezger to bite my head off?

As it turned out, I didn't have to worry. Marf and Ezger were waiting for me in the corner where I'd eaten lunch with Ila the day before. As I walked over to them with Hooree, Marf held up Ila's screen for me to take.

"I am so sorry," she said. "I accidentally left your house while holding this in my hand."

"That was not an accident!" Ezger snarled at her. "You stole it."

"Be quiet, Ezger. I am trying to be polite."

"I'm just glad I got it back. Thank you for bringing it to me!" I put Ila's screen in my bag, pulled out my lunch, and sat down next to Marf. She was taking up four Zhuri-sized stools.

Hooree stared at Marf with his giant compound eyes. "You went to the human's home?"

"Yes," said Marf. "We are plotting a very daring robbery of Choom's largest bank."

Choom has banks? I thought as Hooree drew his head back in what looked like horror.

"It's not true!" I said quickly. "She's just making a joke."

"People should not make jokes," Hooree whined. "It causes smell."

"I don't make smells," Marf told him. "And people should not sit near me if they don't like jokes. Because I tell a lot of them."

Hooree glared at her, then turned to me. "If you wish to eat your nutrition with criminals, then they should be your school guides instead of me."

"Please don't be upset!" I told him. "I just want to live in peace with everyone."

"It is impossible to live in peace with criminals," he whined. "Everyone knows that." Then he flitted away, leaving a whiff of gasoline in his wake.

Oh geez. "Hooree, wait!" I stood up, fumbling to close my container of Chow so I could follow him.

"You are not choosing his company over ours, are you?" Marf asked.

"I have to! He's my guide." I was having trouble closing my Chow container while still keeping my eyes on Hooree. He was headed for the faucets of food. A few more seconds, and I'd lose him for good in the thick crowd of Zhuri.

"We can be your guides," said Marf.

"You're not in my class," I said. I finally managed to close the Chow container. Hooree was so far away now that I was going to have to run to catch up with him.

"I am in your class," Ezger said.

"You *are*?" I turned to look at him, completely losing track of Hooree.

"Yes. Yurinuri. Six None Six. Yesterday, I was the one who asked if you ate other humans."

"Ohmygosh! I'm so sorry!" I studied Ezger's face, trying to memorize his features so I wouldn't make such an embarrassing mistake again. "Why didn't you say hello this morning?"

"I didn't want to. And stop staring at me like that."

"Sorry!" I was getting even more embarrassed.

"For a Krik, Ezger is very friendly," Marf explained. "But for most other species, he is not friendly at all. So can we be your guides?"

"I don't know if that's a good idea."

"Because we are criminals?"

"No! Of course not!" *Actually, yes.* "It's just that . . . I don't want this to sound offensive. . . ."

"Don't worry about that. Whatever you say, we will not be offended. And if we are, Ezger will bite your head off. But you will die instantly with very little pain, so don't worry about that either."

I had no idea how to reply.

"I am joking," Marf explained.

"I knew that."

"No, you didn't," said Ezger. "You looked very frightened. But do not worry. I would never bite off a part of you." He pointed to my container of Chow. "Anyone who eats feces like that could not possibly taste good."

"Why don't we discuss something more pleasant?" Marf suggested.

"Great idea," I agreed. "Speaking of jokes—when the Zhuri think something's funny, do they make a kind of . . . doughnut smell?"

"I do not know what a doughnut is," said Marf. "But if it is sweet, then probably yes. I find the Zhuri laughter smell quite pleasant. It's a shame they are discouraged from making it." Marf lowered her voice. "And *also* speaking of jokes—Ezger and I have some questions for you."

"Okay. Sure! Ask away."

She and Ezger both turned their heads and looked back at my guard, who was sitting a few feet behind us with his weapon in his lap, drinking his lunch.

Ezger lowered his voice too. "We watched the videos that were on your sister's screen. The noises she made, with her mouth and that machine that had strings—what were they?"

"You mean when she was singing? And playing guitar?"

"Please speak more quietly," Marf warned me in a low rumble.

"Sorry."

"Is that what it is called?" Ezger asked. "Singing? Those noises were very pleasing. I liked them a lot."

"I told Ezger that noise is called music," said Marf.

I nodded. "That's right," I said in a half whisper. "And you liked it?" This seemed like fantastic news.

"I liked it very much," said Ezger. "Can you make the music noises?"

"No, sorry," I said. "I don't play guitar. And I sing like a dog howls."

"I do not know what that means."

"Dogs are, um—never mind. It just means I'm a terrible singer."

"I did not care for your sister's music," Marf said, her rumbling voice so low that I worried my translator might not pick it up. "Ororo ears don't enjoy such high frequencies. But I will tell you the thing I *did* like—"

"Which I hated," Ezger interjected.

"Which Ezger hated, because he has very bad taste: the picture story with the flying people."

"*The Birdleys*?"

"Yes!" Marf nodded her head so hard that her whole body shook. "It was very amusing."

"You liked *The Birdleys*? That's amazing!"

"It is a fascinating form of art. It is a series of pictures, yes? And they are combined at speed to give the illusion of movement?"

"Yeah. It's called a cartoon. Some of the funniest human shows ever were cartoons."

"I really enjoyed the cartoon," said Marf.

"I hated it *so* much," Ezger said again.

Marf ignored him. "Did the animals in that cartoon live on your planet with you?"

"Kind of," I said. "I mean, they did—but they weren't like that at all in real life. They're called birds. And real birds had very tiny brains. They didn't talk, or wear clothes, or live in houses—so really, the show was about humans. Everybody on *The Birdleys* looked like a bird, but acted like a human. Does that make sense?"

"Not at all," said Ezger.

"It does to me," said Marf. "Do you have more episodes of this show?"

"Yeah," I said. "I have a bunch."

"May I come to your house after school? I would like to discuss them with you."

"Discuss them?" I asked. "Or watch them?"

"Both."

"Sure. What do you want to discuss?"

Marf turned her head again to look at the guard, who was making slurping noises as he rooted around in his glass for the last drops of his lunch. The guard looked up, making eye contact with her.

"I will tell you later," said Marf.

13

PSST! WANNA BUY A CARTOON?

I DIDN'T EVEN try to understand Yurinuri's lesson that afternoon. I was too excited about my conversation with Marf and Ezger.

Assuming the rest of their species had the same taste they did, it was huge news. If the Ororo liked our TV, and the Krik liked our music, maybe they'd want us to stay on Choom.

And if so, couldn't they help get the Zhuri to change their minds?

By the time class ended, I'd rescued the whole human race in my head by forming a music-and-TV-based alliance with the Ororo and the Krik. When Yurinuri dismissed us, I headed for Ezger, but he and the other Krik raced out the door so fast that they were gone before I reached it.

I was about to follow them into the hallway when Yurinuri called out to me.

"Lan human, may I speak to you for a moment?"

"Yes, sir!" I walked back to the front of the room, and he

lowered his voice so the departing Zhuri kids and my guard couldn't hear him. "Have you given more thought to your presentation?"

"Oh! Yes, sir!" *Actually, no.* So much had happened over the past day that I'd forgotten all about it. "I just, um . . . need a little more time. Do you have any advice about what I should include?"

"As I said before . . ." His voice was almost a whisper. "Some people think the human has positive things to offer our society."

"Okay! Any things in particular, sir? I was just talking to a Krik and an Ororo about comedy and music—"

He interrupted me with a loud whine as he looked over my shoulder. "It should be *educational,* Lan human."

I turned back to see where he was looking. My guard was halfway across the room, flitting toward us.

"The purpose of your presentation is *educational,*" Yurinuri repeated. "Do you understand?"

"Yes, sir." *But not really.*

"Very good. I will see you tomorrow."

When I got to the hallway, it was so packed with Zhuri and Krik that finding Ezger was hopeless. There was also no sign of Marf, who would've been impossible to miss as the only Ororo in the school. I'd been hoping to hitch a ride home in her fancy silver pod, but I wound up taking my usual generic one and sitting in silence with my armed guard as I tried to puzzle out just what the heck my teacher was asking me to do.

"Positive things to offer" seemed like they should include some kind of art, maybe even music or comedy. But the chief servant had called that stuff "poisonous," and just mentioning it had seemed to freak out Yurinuri. Like Marf and Ezger at lunch, he hadn't wanted my guard to hear me talking about it. Plus, he'd insisted that my presentation should be "educational," whatever that meant.

None of it made a whole lot of sense, but I figured I could ask Marf about it if she came over to our house like she'd said she would. Even if we couldn't so much as talk about things like *The Birdleys* in front of the Zhuri, I was still excited about my idea to use them to get the Krik and the Ororo on our side.

When I got home, though, Dad and Ila didn't think the idea was nearly as exciting as I did. They were both lying on the couch. Dad's venom-swollen face and upper body looked even worse than when I'd left that morning.

"If we can get the Krik and the Ororo on our side, won't that help change the Zhuri's minds?"

"It cahn't hurrt," Dad slurred, wincing from the pain of talking with half his face puffed up like a dark red balloon. "Buht the Zhuri urr the onesh in charge."

"Don't talk," Ila told him. "The doctor said you'll just make it worse."

"A doctor came? What did he say?"

"The same thing Leeni said: 'it'll get better.' Except it's not getting better." Ila shook her head. "He gave us medicine to put on the wound, but it just seems to make it swell up more."

"I'm sorry, Dad." He winked at me with his good eye. I guess winking didn't hurt as much as smiling.

"Did you get my screen back?" Ila asked.

"Oh! Yes." I gave it to her, and she disappeared into her bedroom with it like a squirrel running off with a nut.

Then we heard the thunderclap of an incoming pod. It was

Marf. I introduced her to Dad, and the first thing she said after fixing his translator was, "You need medicine for your injury."

"They gave him some," I told her. "But it doesn't help."

"Zhuri doctors are not competent to care for non-Zhuri species," she said. "Why don't you come to our home this evening? My parents can make the medicine that you need. You can also eat our evening meal with us. Humans enjoy Ororo food, don't they?"

"Yesh! Wonnerful! Thahnk you!" said Dad, trying to smile through the pain.

"How much will this cost us?" I asked.

"Lahn!"

Dad glared at me, but Marf just grinned. "It is a fair question. I am a businessperson. But there is no charge. Consider it payment for the pleasure I got from watching human television on your sister's screen."

"So what did you want to discuss about the *Birdleys*?"

"Nothing," said Marf. "It was not important. But I will happily watch more episodes if you have them."

"Sure. But shouldn't we go to your place first and get Dad's face fixed?"

"Cahn we wait thill my wife comesh home?" Dad slurred.

"Oh! Yeah. My mom would definitely want to come with us. She should be home in a little while. Is that okay?"

"We can leave whenever you wish," Marf replied. "There is no hurry."

The three of us sat down on the couch, and I took out my screen to show Marf another *Birdleys* episode. But she didn't think the display was big enough, so she fetched some tools from her pod and used them to add a transmitter to my screen that let me cast the *Birdleys* video to the big Zhuri television on the wall.

It was the kind of project that probably would've taken a human technician days to pull off, even with the right parts. But Marf managed it in about three minutes. As he watched her work, Dad looked amazed.

"The average Ororo is seven thousand times as smart as the average human," I explained, repeating what Marf had told me.

"I guessh sho," Dad slurred.

After Marf set up the screencast, the three of us watched a couple of *Birdleys* episodes. Marf cracked up constantly, and I found out Ororo laugh almost the same way humans do—she didn't make much noise, but her eyes crinkled up, and her body shook in a bouncy jiggle that almost knocked me off the couch once.

"You really understand all of these jokes?" I asked.

"Not all the words. But the movements, of course. It is just physics. He wants to go over the wall. But he goes through it instead. And intention—he wants it to be quiet. But his mate has invited her loud friend to their home."

"This is my favorite show. Like, ever."

"The birds remind me of Zhuri. Both in the way they move and in their thinking. They are very proud, but their actions are often foolish."

After the second episode, Dad excused himself to clean up before dinner. As soon as he left, Marf turned to me.

"Now we must have a serious discussion."

"About what?"

"*The Birdleys.* I have a business proposal for you. But first you

131

must promise never to speak a word about it. Especially to your parents."

"Why not?"

"Because if human parents are like Ororo parents, they will ruin everything."

"Oh. Okay. So what is it?"

"You swear you will not discuss this? With your parents, or anyone else?"

"Yes! Sure."

"You will keep it a secret? On pain of death?"

"Death?"

"If you keep the secret, it won't come to that. Do you promise?"

"I . . . uh . . . this whole death thing . . . ?"

"Forget that I said death. Just promise you will keep the secret."

"But you wouldn't . . . actually kill me, right?"

"It's very unlikely. You are the only non-Ororo I have ever heard tell a joke. It wasn't very funny, but it showed potential. That is a rare and valuable thing on this planet. *No one* around here is funny. Except other Ororo. But their sense of humor is very dark. Sometimes, they just make me sad instead of amused."

"What about Ezger? Isn't he funny?"

"Not on purpose. Ezger's jokes are mostly accidental. Although he is quite good at sarcasm. . . . We're getting distracted here. Back to *The Birdleys*: How many episodes are there?"

"I don't know. A few hundred? It was a really popular show on Earth."

"I wish to buy all of them from you."

"Really? Wow! Okay. But . . . you can just come over and watch them for free."

"I prefer to possess them. Are they all on your screen?"

"No, I just have a few. Most of them are in the archive up on the human ship. At least, I think they have all of them up there. Why do you want to buy them?"

"That is not important."

"Are you going to, like, sell them to other Ororo? Because here's the thing. . . ." I explained my idea about getting the Ororo and the Krik interested in human TV and music, then asking them to help us win over the Zhuri.

Marf shook her head. "Your plan is mathematically unsound."

"What do you mean?"

"Planet Choom is democratic. Roughly speaking, each person has an equal voice."

"So that's good. Right?"

"It depends on which species you are. There are six billion Zhuri, ten million Krik, and just two thousand Ororo. Mathematically speaking, the Ororo and Krik's opinions do not matter at all."

"But the Zhuri must care a little bit what you think."

"They do not."

"Not at all?"

"No. I am sorry. All the most important decisions are made by Zhuri alone."

"Oh." I sighed. So much for saving the human race through comedy.

"Will you sell the episodes to me?" she asked again.

I thought about it. "Maybe. But why does this have to be such a big secret?"

"There is risk involved."

"What kind of risk?"

"These videos are illegal."

"They *are*?"

"Yes. Unless they are educational."

"Oh! That explains it." I told her about my conversation with my teacher and the "educational" presentation he wanted me to do.

"Do you think *The Birdleys* are educational?" I asked.

Marf shook her head. "No. They are entertainment—their purpose is to create emotion. Laughter, joy, sorrow . . ."

"I don't know about sorrow."

"The episode where Duane lost his job was quite sad in spots."

"That's true. And they're *definitely* meant to create laughter."

"Then they are unfortunately illegal. You should not let any Zhuri know they exist. And no one can ever know I purchased them from you. I will pay you four hundred rhee per episode."

"Wait—how illegal are they? Like, should I not even *have* them?"

"The government would definitely not approve. But distributing them is *much* more illegal than having them. This is why you cannot tell anyone you sold them to me, on pain of death."

"I thought we took death off the table."

"You did. *I* didn't. I only said it was unlikely. But if you ever tell anyone about this conversation, I will be forced to kill you instantly. And it will be a very painful death. You will scream and beg for mercy. Which I will not give you."

"You're joking."

"It's possible. I *did* say that Ororo have a very dark sense of humor. But just to be on the safe side, don't tell anyone about this conversation. Or about the fact that you're selling all the *Birdleys* episodes to me."

I thought about it for a moment. "I'm sorry—but if they're that illegal, I can't sell them to you. The government's already looking for a reason to kick us off the planet. If somebody got busted with *Birdleys* episodes, it'd be obvious they came from us. So I'd pretty much be destroying the whole human race."

Marf nodded rapidly, her skin rippling from the movement. "That is fine. I completely understand. Please forget I ever said anything about buying the videos, and don't speak of this to anyone." She patted me on the leg. "Also, dinner is no longer free. Let's watch another episode."

"Wait—dinner's not free anymore?"

"Of course not. That was a promotional offer, designed to influence your decision in selling me the videos. If you still wish to eat Ororo food at our house, you will have to pay me a thousand rhee. Plus five thousand for your father's medicine."

"Oh . . ." A sinking feeling started to spread in my stomach. "The thing is, I don't think we actually *have* money? So . . ."

The corners of Marf's big dark eyes crinkled in a smile. "I thought you could tell when I was joking."

"I can! Some of the time."

"Don't worry. We will give you the medicine for free. And the dinner too."

"Thank you so much! Hey—if you let us take home the left-overs? I'll give you all the *Birdleys* episodes for free. And you can sell them to anybody you want."

Marf's eyes widened. "Is this true?"

It was my turn to smile. "Of course not! Can't *you* tell when *I'm* joking?"

Marf smiled back, even wider. "I enjoy your company, Lan human. It will be a real shame when I am forced to kill you."

"I know, right? Hey, in all seriousness—should I delete these *Birdleys* episodes from my screen? Like, would the government kick us off the planet just for having them?"

Marf shook her enormous head. "Don't worry about that. At least not until I've seen all the episodes. Please, play another one."

I cued up the next episode and settled back into the auto-massaging couch, feeling more hopeful than usual about Planet Choom. The news about *The Birdleys* being illegal was a little scary, but I felt like I had at least one superintelligent giant marshmallow on my side.

Until she killed me.

But I was 98 percent sure she was joking about that.

Or maybe just 95 percent. Either way, my odds were pretty good.

FOOD FOR THOUGHT

AFTER MOM GOT home, tired and aching from a long day at the morgue, we all put on our best outfits, and Marf led us out the door and across the red lawn to her pod. As we approached it, the door hovered open in a dramatic-sounding *whoosh*.

Mom paused at the threshold and peered inside. The roomy interior was covered from floor to ceiling with some kind of luxurious-looking fuzzy purple fabric, and the seats gently rippled with the same auto-massaging substance as our beds and couch.

"Oh my," said Mom. "This is quite a ship."

"*YEEHEEHEE . . . !*"

"STOP! YOU CANNOT BOARD THIS POD WITHOUT APPROVAL!"

The two guards from the front of our house were flitting toward us, weapons at the ready.

"I am so sorry—" Mom began to say.

"They have approval," said Marf, talking over her. "Please check your assignment roster."

One of the guards flitted over to their much plainer pod, parked by the side of the house. He opened the door and checked a screen inside. Then he called out to his partner:

"The Ororo is correct. The humans have been authorized to attend evening nutrition in Lot Seven Nine Nine."

"We will have to escort you," his partner told us.

"I am sorry, but there is not enough room in my pod," said Marf, practically shoving us all inside. "You may follow behind me."

Without waiting for an answer, Marf shut the pod door on the guards and pressed a button on the control panel. Instantly the pod shot fifty yards straight up, passing through the fence with an even more explosive *BZZZZZT!* than usual.

It stopped as fast as it took off, hovering in midair for half a second. I had just enough time to look down and see the guards below us racing for their own pod before we took off again like a rocket.

Moments later, we were hurtling over the city so fast that the buildings passed by in a blur. The strangest thing about it was that nothing inside the pod was affected by the sudden changes in speed. When it leaped into the air, we should've all been flattened to the floor—but I didn't feel more than a soft flutter in my stomach. And when the pod zoomed away, I would've expected us to be knocked backward like bowling pins against the rear wall. Instead, there wasn't even a mild lurch.

My family was as bewildered as I was.

"How is it," Mom asked, "that this pod seems to defy physics?"

"The technology is called 'inertial buffering.' It is difficult to explain in a way you would understand," Marf told her.

"Ororo are seven thousand times smarter than humans," I explained to Mom.

She nodded. "Interesting. And how did you get authorization for us to go to dinner at your house?" she asked Marf.

"That is also difficult to explain," said Marf. I suspected she'd gotten the authorization the same way she'd gotten the clearance code that allowed her pod to cross our fence—in other words, illegally—but I kept my mouth shut. As scared as I was of the Zhuri government, I didn't want to risk missing an Ororo meal.

Besides, now that we were in the air, if we'd broken the law, it was too late to do anything about it.

Ila sank into one of the massaging chairs and looked around. It hadn't taken much convincing to get her to leave the house once we'd explained that we'd be eating Ororo food. "This is a *really* nice pod," she said.

"Thank you!" Marf beamed. "I paid for it myself. I am a businessperson."

"Really? What kind of business?"

"I sell things. Mostly small gadgets and toy robots that I've made."

And illegal videos . . . if I'd let her, I thought as Marf lumbered to the rear of the pod and opened a small cabinet door along the bottom of the back wall. A two-foot-tall Krik replica made of silver steel poked its head out of the cabinet. Ila was the closest to it, and she yelped in surprise, stumbling backward as the Krik robot moved toward us, snapping its jaws and growling.

"Don't be afraid," Marf told Ila. "It only eats metal."

She reached into a dish on the control panel, picked up a

tiny circuit board, and tossed it at the robot, which jumped up to catch it in midair. It chomped down on the board, chewing noisily as it retreated back into its cabinet.

"Wow," said Ila.

"My friend Ezger does not like my robots," Marf said. "He is a Krik, and he thinks I am making fun of his species with them." Marf paused. "Of course, he's entirely correct."

"Is it common for Ororo and Krik to be friends?" Mom asked. "I'd been told there were some . . . issues between your people."

"You mean that they were fond of eating us?"

"Yes. That seems like a real obstacle to healthy relations."

"It was at first. But the Ororo solved it many generations ago. We genetically manipulated our fat cells to render them poisonous to the Krik. Now, if a Krik eats any part of an Ororo, it will die instantly."

"Is this another joke?" I asked.

"Not at all. It was a creative solution to a serious public health problem."

Just as suddenly and smoothly as it had rocketed up to speed, the pod came to a stop, and we descended into an Ororo subdivision that looked exactly like the one we lived in, except that all the houses seemed to have people living in them.

"And here we are," said Marf with a smile. "I wonder how long it will take your guards to catch up to us."

MARF'S HOUSE WAS identical to ours . . . if ours had been taken over by mad scientists who'd installed wild-looking gadgets and machinery everywhere. Her parents, Ulf and Hunf, looked just like Marf, except older, larger, and less blue-tinged.

"Welcome to our home," said Ulf, the mother. My translator gave her a warm, pleasant, suburban-mom-on-an-old-TV-show voice signature. "We were very pleased when Marf messaged us that you would be eating here tonight."

Hunf's signature was an older man's slow drawl. "I hope our daughter didn't try to charge you money for the food," he said with a sideways glance at Marf.

"No! Not at all," Mom assured them.

Hunf turned to Dad. "Before we eat," he said, "would you like an antidote for your venom poisoning?"

"I'd lurrv thaht," slurred Dad.

In the space of ten minutes, Hunf scraped a DNA sample from Dad's tongue, analyzed it, designed a medicinal cream that would counteract the venom without side effects, and manufactured eight ounces of it using some kind of biochemical kiln the size of a shoebox.

Dad rubbed some of the cream into his skin, and the bright red swelling began to go down almost immediately. By the time we sat down to dinner a few minutes later, his left eye had reopened, and he could talk and eat normally again.

"I can't tell you how much I appreciate this," he told Hunf.

"It was trivial," Hunf replied. "When you leave, you should bring the rest of the cream with you."

"Do I need to keep using it?"

"No. But you will need it when you're attacked again."

When? Our eyes all widened. But before Dad could ask a follow-up question, Ulf ushered us to the table.

"Why don't we eat?" she suggested.

THE MEAL WAS even more delicious than our last experience with Ororo food. There were twenty different flavors, and more of each one than we could possibly finish. We did our best not to eat like starving dogs, but we probably failed.

Ulf and Hunf didn't seem to mind. "You should take the leftovers home with you," Ulf said.

"Thank you so much!" Mom gushed. "We are very grateful to you for your kindness."

We all echoed her. "Yes, thank you!"

"Thank you so much!"

"This is wonderful! Thank you!"

"It is trivial," Ulf said. "But you are welcome. Your situation is difficult, and we are glad to help."

"I am wondering," Mom asked, "if you have any advice for us? We could benefit greatly from your wisdom."

"What do you wish to know?"

"How to persuade the Zhuri that we are peaceful, so they will allow humans to stay here."

"But you are not peaceful," Ulf said.

Mom didn't expect to hear that. None of us did.

"We *are* peaceful," she insisted.

"As individuals, perhaps," said Hunf. "Not as a species. You destroyed your home planet. What could be more violent than that?"

"But we've learned from this tragedy. And we have renounced violence, now and in the future."

"You may wish that to be so," said Hunf. "You may even believe it. But it isn't true. Your species simply hasn't reached that stage of social and emotional development."

"In our case," Ulf explained, "it took the Ororo more than a thousand generations to fully abandon our violent instincts."

"Yet even now," added Hunf, "I still wish to remove the wings of any Zhuri who parks his pod in my assigned space."

"My husband is joking," said Ulf.

"Only a little," Hunf said.

"I don't believe humans are incapable of change," Dad announced.

"I don't believe that either," Hunf replied. "But such fundamental change rarely happens quickly. Humans are likely to be violent for many generations to come. But that is not the true obstacle to your finding a home on Planet Choom. The Krik and the Zhuri both have violent tendencies, yet they manage to live in peace. And Zhuri weapons technology is far superior to yours—human violence is no real threat to them. It's simply the excuse they have chosen to justify denying you refuge."

"But why?" Mom asked. "If they don't fear our violence, then why do they wish to keep us out?"

"Because they fear the emotions you might create among their people," Ulf said.

"That is the primary reason," Hunf agreed. "But there is also an element of genuine concern for your own safety. The Zhuri are very fearful of causing another tragedy like the one that befell the Nug."

The four of us looked at each other. Mom said what was on all our minds. "What *did* happen to the Nug? I've asked this question many times, but I've never gotten an answer."

The Ororo's eyes all widened. "Oh dear," said Ulf. "No one told you about the Nug?" Her enormous head swiveled to look at her husband.

Hunf let out a deep, rumbling sigh. Then he pushed his chair back and rose heavily to his feet.

"When you finish your food," he said, "please join me on the couch. This will be easier to understand if you see the video."

15

SOMETIMES HISTORY
ISN'T PRETTY

THE MASSIVE ORORO couch was big enough for all seven of us. Ulf and Hunf sat on the far ends, with Marf next to her father and my family wedged in the middle, looking (and, at least for me, feeling) like little children alongside the giant Ororo. Using a remote control, Ulf clicked through the interface of a Zhuri video library on the wall-sized TV screen as Hunf lectured to us.

"In most societies," he explained, "there are two basic forces in conflict: progress and tradition. They battle for political control. When progress has the upper hand, there is growth and change. But when that change comes too quickly or causes problems, tradition takes over to act as a stabilizing force.

"The Zhuri—who rule Choom because they outnumber the Ororo and Krik six hundred to one—are a hive species. Their biology makes cooperation sacred to them. They can't stand the thought of conflict. Perhaps you've noticed their strange insistence that 'everyone agrees' about everything?"

We all nodded. "Oh, sure."

"That doesn't mean there *isn't* conflict. It just means the Zhuri pretend it doesn't exist. When the traditionalists are in control, as they are now, everyone claims to agree with them about everything . . . until the situation is reversed, the forces of progress take over, and suddenly everyone's in full agreement with the exact opposite of what they agreed the week before."

Ulf interrupted him. "I've found the video, dearest."

"Don't play it yet, my precious. I haven't finished lecturing our guests like a pompous know-it-all." Hunf smiled at us as he narrowed his giant eyes in what looked like a wink, then continued. "Twenty-odd years ago, the progressives had been in charge of Choom's government for nearly a century. They received a distress call from the Nug, who were being driven from their home planet by an invader. The government offered them refuge here. Such offers have been a matter of policy since the Zhuri themselves arrived as refugees a thousand years ago.

"But they didn't simply invite the Nug out of kindness. The government also believed they had something valuable to offer Choom's society. The Nug prided themselves on their performing arts. Song and dance in particular were vital to their culture. The Zhuri had very little experience with that sort of thing."

"They're awfully boring in that way," Marf piped up.

Hunf nodded in agreement with his daughter. "It's true. As a species, they're quite dull. No music, dance, drama, architecture, painting, sculpture—they just plod through life and lay eggs, really. But they'd begun to see this as a shortcoming in themselves. Partly, that's because we Ororo had been living among them for a while, and they'd seen how much art and culture improved our own quality of life. We've always had tons of it. But when we immigrated to Choom, we didn't share our art with the

Zhuri, because they clearly had no taste for it. We even kept our television system separate from theirs."

"Ororo television has dozens of channels," Marf chimed in. "But no one can watch them except us."

"It's for the best," said Ulf. "Some of our programming seems quite strange to non-Ororo. It even seems strange to me sometimes."

"So the Nug arrived on Choom," Hunf continued, "eager to share their art with the Zhuri—and the Nug weren't boring at all! Quite the opposite. They held festivals of dance that lasted for days."

"We didn't care for the Nug's dancing," Ulf said. "We can move if we have to, but we're more of a couch species. The Zhuri were quite taken with it, though. It turned out they had a real knack for mass dancing. For them, it was like their swarming behavior, only positive—joyful instead of violent. At first it seemed as if the Nug might trigger a real transformation in Zhuri society."

"But then"—Hunf raised his hand in a dramatic gesture— "the Nug held their Festival of Wailing."

At the mention of it, all three Ororo sighed heavily.

"It was one of their oldest traditions," said Hunf. "They held one every five years, for ten days at a time. And it was *horrendous*."

"I've cued it up on the TV," Ulf said. "Would you like to see a bit of it?"

"Of course! Please," said Mom.

Ulf pressed a button on her remote. On the wall screen, a vast plaza appeared in the heart of a Choom city, surrounded by the usual honeycomb-shaped beige buildings. The space between them was black, wet, and roiling. It looked like a stormy ocean of oil.

Then the noise hit me—an earsplitting shriek so painful that I clapped my hands over my ears. Even with them covered, the noise was so loud and aggravating that it started to make me nauseous. The rest of my family had the same reaction:

"OW!"

"AAAAGH!"

"PLEASE, STOP!"

Ulf paused the video and pointed at the screen with the remote. "All the Nug on the planet—every single one—gathered in the middle of the city and slithered all over each other while they screamed their heads off."

I stared closely at the screen. What I'd thought was a huge pool of black liquid turned out to be a writhing pile of giant, wormlike Nug.

"And this Festival of Wailing went on for ten *days*?" Dad asked. "That horrible noise lasted ten whole days?"

"It would have," said Hunf. "Except that on the fourth day, a swarm of angry Zhuri killed every last Nug."

Mom gasped. I'm pretty sure I did too, but the noise was drowned out by Ila's high-pitched whimper.

"It wasn't intentional," said Ulf. "Even the Zhuri who were in the swarm probably didn't set out to cause a massacre. I don't mean to excuse what they did, because intentional or not, it was monstrous—but it's very difficult to explain in words just how painful the Festival of Wailing was for everyone but the Nug. We lived miles away, and even at that distance, their screams were so intolerable that they made us physically ill."

"The sounds were even more painful to the Zhuri," Hunf said. "And the government did everything it could to persuade the Nug to stop. But once they were locked into their ritual, it was impossible to talk to them, let alone get them to quit screaming."

"The government did its best to stop the swarm from forming too," added Ulf. "But the Zhuri are a hive species—once their swarms get going, they take on a life of their own."

"Even in a non-hive species," said Hunf, "large groups of people—especially angry or frightened ones—behave in ways individuals never would. Sometimes they wind up doing things that are incredibly tragic and stupid. Not to mention violent. That's what happened here. It was a kind of mass sickness. And when it was over, the Zhuri were *horrified* at themselves. They'd invited a whole species to their planet, with the best of intentions, thinking they were doing the Nug a great kindness . . . only to see an angry mob of their own people slaughter them in a fit of rage. Within days, Choom's government had changed hands, and the traditionalists took over."

"It made sense," said Ulf. "When your government's policies have caused a massacre, accidental or not, it's wise to change course." She shook her head. "But then they started this silly business of trying to suppress emotion."

"Zhuri swarms are triggered by the anger smell," Hunf explained. "And the government wanted to stop swarms from ever forming again. But they somehow got it in their heads that the best way to do that would be to suppress *all* smells. They thought if they could just shut down their whole society's emotional responses, the result would be peace and agreement forever."

"It's completely misguided, of course," said Ulf. "And doomed

149

to fail, eventually. The Zhuri aren't terribly emotional to begin with—but even so, they can't eliminate their emotions any more than we can. Still, I suspect they'll keep plodding along with that stupid policy for a few more decades, because they really do believe it's the best thing for the planet. The poor fools."

"So where does that leave humans?" Mom asked.

"Not in a good place at all, I'm afraid," said Ulf. "The progressive government invited you here. But the traditionalists are in charge now. And if your great achievement as a species is art—well, that just terrifies them, because it's the same thing the Nug said, and look how that turned out. So they want you gone."

"But they're conflicted," Hunf added, "because the government *did* invite you here—and they can't bear to think they might be responsible for the demise of a second species. So they've decided to play up your violence as a way of putting all the blame on you for things not working out."

"Is that why the television keeps showing images of human wars?" Dad asked.

"Of course. As long as 'everyone agrees' you're a threat to their safety, the public will demand your removal. The government can get rid of you without feeling as if they've broken their promise."

We were silent for a minute, trying to work out what all of this meant.

"So what can we do," Mom finally asked, "except try to hold out until the government changes hands again?"

Hunf shook his head. "I'm afraid that's impossible. There's some whispered disagreement here and there with the government—there always is—but nothing like what it would take for power to change hands. Zhuri governments tend to last a hundred years or more. This one's been in power for less than twenty. You can't hold out for eighty years—in your situation, even eighty days would be a miracle. I hate to say it, but I don't think you've got long at all."

Ulf reached out and patted Mom on the leg with her giant hand. "We're terribly sorry. You seem like a nice species. It's just very bad timing."

"Best of luck to you, though," added Hunf. "Have you tried any other planets?"

IT WAS TOUGH to keep the conversation going after that, because my whole family was too shocked and depressed for small talk. A few minutes later, our two armed guards knocked on the door—they'd finally caught up after Marf had ditched them back at our place—and we decided to get a ride home from them in their pod. Before we left, Ulf and Hunf gave us enough Ororo food to last a couple of days.

"If you ever need more," Ulf said, "just let Marf know. And *don't* let her charge you for it."

We thanked them for being so generous, but I couldn't help wondering if they'd only given us a couple of days' worth because they didn't think we'd be here any longer than that.

Once we were airborne in a standard-issue pod, which felt dreary and slow after Marf's luxury rocket ride, Ila turned off her translator so the guards couldn't understand her.

"Are we going to leave now," she asked Mom with an edge in her voice, "or are we just going to wait for them to kill us?"

Mom turned off her own translator. "Nobody's going to kill anybody."

"How can you say that? They swarmed us the second we got here! How long before we end up like those poor worms?"

I switched off my own translator. "That was different. The Nug's screams were *hurting* people. We're not hurting anybody."

Ila just snorted and shook her head.

"Lan's right," Mom said. "And we've got things to offer them too. When we were negotiating with the Zhuri before we left Mars, they were *so* excited about our art. I bet a lot of them still are. It's just that now their government doesn't want them exposed to it."

"Marf told me it's illegal to spread videos that cause emotion," I said. "Like, if we sold a *Birdleys* episode to people, that'd be illegal. Because they're meant to be funny."

"Well, that's a problem, isn't it?" Ila snarled.

"Just videos, though, right?" Dad asked me. "It's not illegal to *cause* emotions—it's just illegal to sell a video that *tries* to cause them?"

I shrugged. "I think so? Maybe?"

"There's got to be a way around that," Mom said.

"I'm pretty sure the Zhuri like to laugh," I said. "Even though it's not polite."

Mom looked at me. "Really? Say more."

"The kids in my class laughed at me today in school. When I tripped over something. They made this really sweet doughnut smell."

"*YEEEHEEEEEEE.*" One of the guards flitted up off his seat.

"He wants us to turn our translators back on," said Dad.

The guard lifted his pronged weapon just enough to get his point across.

"Maybe you should try to make them laugh," Mom told me before she turned on her translator. "Just don't put it in a video."

16

THE SWEET STINK
OF SLAPSTICK

ILA WOULDN'T GET out of bed the next morning. When Mom and Dad couldn't rouse her, they sent me into her bedroom to take a shot at it.

She was on her side, curled up in a ball. Her arms were clasped together and bent in front of her chest like she was pray-ing. I could see the little ripples of the mattress gently massaging her bottom arm.

"C'mon, Ila, let's go to school. Iruu was really disappointed when you weren't there yesterday. If you don't show up, he's going to take it personally."

She opened her eyes, but she didn't move. "They would've killed me," she said.

"What?"

"If I'd sung when we landed. Like Mom and Dad wanted me to. The Zhuri would've killed me. Just like they killed the Nug."

"That's ridiculous! The Nug weren't singing. They were *screaming.* It was like they were stabbing people in the ear. Your voice is beautiful. The Zhuri would've been thrilled if you sang. I bet they *still* would."

"No, they wouldn't."

"Yes, they would! Did you know Marf and Ezger watched your *Pop Singer* videos? They *loved* them." It was only half-true, but I figured Marf would cover for me if Ila asked.

Ila raised her head a little. "When did they watch them?"

"The other day. When Marf took your screen home."

For a moment I thought she was going to get up. But then she let her head sink back onto the mattress.

"It doesn't matter. They're not Zhuri."

After that, nothing I said could get my sister to move. In the end I went to school alone again.

WHEN I GOT into the pod with the two guards, one of them made a little flitting motion, like he was excited to see I was alone. The other one hung his head.

"Does this mean you get the day off, sir?" I asked the flitter.

He didn't answer me, but the other one let off a little whiff of anger, and I knew I was right.

Halfway to school, my phone beeped with a message from Naya:

R U being a good doggie?

I messaged back:

SUCH a good doggie! I have been licking everybody's face

The transport must've been orbiting right above us, or close to it, because her reply showed up just a few seconds later, and we started an almost-in-real-time conversation:

Eeew that is gross mental image what do their compound eyes taste like?

Raspberries with a little hint of nachos

MIND BLOWN

tbh I have not actually licked anybody pretty sure it is considered rude

Srsly tho how is it going???

Mom had warned me more than once to stay positive when I talked to anybody on the ship, so I couldn't type *The government wants to get rid of us, the TV news lies about us 24/7, somebody puked poisonous venom on Dad, there are protestors everywhere, and my sister won't get out of bed because she's sure they're going to kill us.*

But I didn't want to lie to my best friend. So I tried to turn the conversation back to Naya:

It's ok. I've made one good friend so far—an Ororo

(They are the giant marshmallow-looking people)

How are you??? What's going on up there???

Honestly?

When I saw that one-word reply, it kicked up a little flutter of fear in my stomach. Then Naya's next message came through, and the flutter got ten times worse:

It's getting bad up here

People r scared and angry

Feels like it did before the food riot

That was the last thing I wanted to hear. I stared at her words for so long without replying that Naya sent another message:

Sorry don't mean to freak you out

We'll be okay

I realized I was being the opposite of positive by not answering, so I sent a flurry of replies back:

No it's fine

I'm so sorry to hear that

DO NOT WORRY

We're going to win them over and make this work

They will let u all land if I have to lick every single Zhuri to make it happen

RUFF RUFF DO NOT WORRY WE GOT THIS!!!

Then it was my turn to stare at the screen while I waited for Naya to reply.

OK cool I know you will do great

WHO'S A GOOD DOGGIE?

LAN'S A GOOD DOGGIE!

Keep on lickin' ruff ruff I love you

The scariest part of the whole message was the *I love you*. Naya wasn't the type to get emotional like that unless she was seriously freaked out. I ended the conversation with:

Love you too almost at school now g2g bye!!!

SERIOUSLY DON'T WORRY WE GOT THIS!!!

Then I put my screen away and tried not to think about what would happen if we failed and the Zhuri threw us out.

IRUU MET ME in the lobby. "Good morning, Lan!" he said. "Is Ila not coming again today?"

The cartoon-frog sound of his voice signature made me smile. "Hello, Iruu! It is great to see you! I am so sorry, but Ila stayed home. She is not feeling well."

He hung his head. "I am sorry too. It pleases me to be helpful to her. I also receive extra credit for it from my learning specialist."

I looked around. "Have you seen Hooree?"

"Not today, no. Do *you* need help finding your class?"

"Would you receive extra credit if you escorted me instead?"

"Yes, I would."

"Then please do! It will be very helpful to me!"

"Thank you!"

I didn't need the help, but I was glad for Iruu's company, even if he was getting bribed to provide it. It was nice knowing at least one Zhuri in the school was willing to talk to me.

"Can I ask you a question, Iruu?" My guard was trailing behind us as we walked down the crowded hallway, and the whine of other voices was loud enough that I didn't think he could hear our conversation.

"Of course! Answering questions is what guides are for."

"Do you like to laugh?"

"Some people think laughter is okay."

"But what do *you* think?"

"I think . . ." He rubbed his wings together. "That I agree with those people," he said in a low whine.

"And . . . what percentage of all the Zhuri on the planet . . . do you think would also agree?"

The wing rubbing got a lot worse. "Everyone agrees—that is, some people—I think—some people think—"

"Never mind! I'm sorry if it was a difficult question." He looked very uncomfortable, and I didn't want to make him upset. Besides, we'd reached my classroom door. "Thank you so much for walking me to class!"

"You are very welcome!" Iruu stopped rubbing his wings and

folded them against his back. It looked like the Zhuri equivalent of a big sigh of relief.

"Goodbye! I hope to see you at lunch!" I started to walk into my class, but he stopped me with a loud whine.

"Lan human?"

"Yes, Iruu?"

"Some of our learning specialists say it is good to ask questions. Even if they are hard to answer."

"Thank you for saying that, Iruu! You are a good friend." I smiled at him, and he flitted up off his feet a couple of inches in response.

That made me feel good, but the feeling didn't last long. As I walked to my seat, I tried to make eye contact and smile at all my classmates. They all ignored me except for Ezger, who grunted in reply when I said hello. Just before I sat down, I caught Hooree's eye, and he rubbed his wings together and turned away.

The lesson began, and Yurinuri picked up where he'd left off the morning before, using his laser marker to write a totally incomprehensible math equation on the wall screen. "Who would like to solve this for urm?" he asked the class.

A Zhuri kid raised his hand, and as I watched him bounce-walk up to the front of the class, wriggle his head, and scratch out an answer, a thought occurred to me.

What if I do that?

It seemed absurdly simple to imitate a Zhuri. And it might be hilarious.

At least, it might be to a human. Would the Zhuri find it funny? Would they make that fresh-baked doughnut smell?

I watched as a few more Zhuri kids bounced up to the front of the room to write on the screen, then either flitted back to their stools with pride or hung their heads in shame.

If I went up there, I had no prayer of getting the answer right. I didn't even know what the questions meant.

Maybe I could make that part funny too.

Try to make them laugh. That's what Mom had said.

The more I thought about raising my hand, the more scared I got. It seemed like a long shot. And if it backfired on me, I might get in serious trouble.

Then again, if there was one place where it might be okay to screw up, it was probably in Yurinuri's class. He seemed like he wanted me to succeed, and he'd probably forgive a mistake if it wasn't too enormous.

I decided to take my chances. When Yurinuri drew the next equation on the screen, I put my hand in the air. He drew his head back in surprise.

"Lan human? Can you solve for urm?"

"I can try, sir!" I sprang to my feet. Slowly, I walked to the front of the room, taking long strides and bending my knees deep with each one, then bobbing up with a little hitch like the Zhuri did.

I heard a low whine of whispers behind me, but no smells. They didn't seem to be getting the joke.

Yurinuri handed me the laser marker. I stood in front of the screen, staring at the meaningless squiggles and slashes of Zhuri math.

Now what?

I drew a stick-figure head with squiggly hair and slashes for its eyes and mouth.

"What is it doing?" someone called out behind me.

"That is not even a number!" whined someone else.

I drew a cartoon of an Ororo, then a Krik with giant, ridiculous-looking teeth.

There was no smell of anything in the air. It wasn't working. My face turned hot with embarrassment.

"I do not think you are understanding the lesson, Lan human," said Yurinuri.

I handed back the laser marker. "I am so sorry! Everyone must agree I am not good at this."

"Everyone also agrees it is important to try," Yurinuri said. "Thank you for doing so. Please take your seat now."

As I turned back to the class, I caught a whiff of the doughnut smell.

Somebody—maybe just one of them—was laughing at me.

I started back toward my stool, hanging my head in exaggerated disappointment as I aped the bouncy Zhuri walk again.

There were more low whines of whispered chatter.

Another hint of the doughnut smell reached my nose.

It's working!

I was just a couple of strides away from my stool. A Zhuri kid was sitting to the left and in front of me. His long, thin legs were stretched out, just barely poking into my path.

They loved it when I tripped yesterday. It was the oldest, dumbest, easiest laugh in the universe.

I went for it.

On my next stride, I brought my foot down just in front of the kid's leg. He started to lift it up to get out of my way, but I quickly sped up my bouncy step, raising my foot and dragging it across his leg just as he lifted it.

Gravity and physics took over. I lost my balance, windmilled my arms, and came crashing down across my stool, flipping it sideways as I hit the floor shoulder first. Fortunately, the floor was the same spongy playground stuff as in our house, or I would've really hurt myself.

Whines of surprise erupted all around me.

"Are you injured, Lan human?" Yurinuri cried out.

I popped up right away, doing my best to seem flustered. "I am so sorry! I am not good at walking either!"

My stool was lying on its side. I set it on its feet and plopped down on it.

Then I breathed in the rich, sugary-sweet smell of Zhuri laughter.

"Clear the air, children," Yurinuri warned them. "We do not want to offend the Lan human. That was an accident."

It wasn't an accident. And I wasn't offended.

I was thrilled.

I made them laugh!

That had to help us somehow. I just needed to figure out the somehow.

17

A PRATFALL TOO FAR

"I HAVE A question," I said as I sat down next to Marf and Ezger in the crowded cafeteria.

"So do I," said Marf. "Where is your sister?"

"Lying in bed."

"Is she unwell?"

"It depends on what you mean by unwell," I said. "She has her good days and her bad days."

"What would make her days better?"

"I don't know. Living back on Earth with a guitar and a music career?"

"I do not understand anything you are saying," said Ezger.

As I got out my leftover Ororo food, Marf stood up. "You will have to excuse me."

"Where are you going?"

"I have an appointment."

"What kind of appointment?" I asked.

She trundled away without an answer. Within a few seconds

she'd crossed the room and disappeared out the door. It was amazing how fast she could move when she wanted to.

"Is Marf mad at me for something?" I asked Ezger.

"Why would she be mad at you?"

"I don't know. She just seemed kind of . . . brisk. Like she was angry."

"I do not think she is angry. It's the opposite. Since she met you, she has been *much* less sad than usual."

Hearing that made me feel delighted and worried at the same time. "Marf's usually sad?"

"She is almost always sad. She is the saddest person I know."

"Why is that?"

"She will tell you it is because all Ororo are sad. But I think it's because she is lonely. Marf is the only Ororo in this whole school. And she is thousands of times smarter than everyone in it. If you ask me, that is a very lonely thing."

"I guess you're right." When I thought about that, it *did* seem awfully lonely.

"Did you have a question? When you sat down?"

"Oh! Yes. Is it illegal to make people laugh?"

"You mean the way you made people laugh in our classroom? When you tripped and fell? Did you do that on purpose?"

I looked over my shoulder at my soldier. He was sitting with his weapon in his lap, sipping his lunch. "Of course not!" I said, making sure I was loud enough for him to hear. "It was an accident. I'm just clumsy."

"It is not illegal to be clumsy," Ezger said. "It is only embarrassing. And most Zhuri will tell you it is very rude to

make people laugh. But that is not the same thing as being illegal."

"Do you like to laugh?" I asked him.

"I don't think so. I have never done it."

"I think it's pretty great."

"It doesn't seem great. When Marf laughs, she looks like she
is having a medical problem."

After that, we ate in silence for a while, except for the noise
of Ezger's lunch smacking him in the face as he chomped down
on it.

As I munched on my Ororo leftovers, I watched the Zhuri
kids waiting in line at the food faucets on the other side of the
room. Most of them stood still, but the more eager ones occasionally flitted their wings, rising up a few inches off the ground.
There were stacks of empty glasses on the shelf behind each
faucet. Once the Zhuri kids had taken a glass and filled it, some
of them loped away on foot to sit on stools, but just as many took
flight, choosing to drink their lunch while hovering in airborne
clusters that clouded the room all the way to the skylit ceiling.

One of the nearby clusters of flying Zhuri seemed to be staring down at me. I was trying to figure out whether I was just
imagining it when a kid detached from the group and zoomed
over to land in front of me. When he got close, I realized it was
Iruu.

"Hello, Lan!"

"Hi, Iruu! Do you know my friend Ezger?"

"I do not," said Iruu.

"I do not either," said Ezger.

They didn't seem interested in getting to know to each other.

I was trying to figure out how to make the situation less awkward when Iruu changed the subject.

"I was told you walked like a Zhuri in class today, and it was very amusing."

"Not on purpose, though!" I lied. "It just kind of happened."

"Can you make it happen again? Can you show me?"

The floating cluster of Zhuri he'd left behind were all still looking down at me. So were a few dozen other Zhuri in the clusters next to them.

I looked across the room. There was a clear path to the nearest faucet.

My heart started to beat faster.

Should I?

I set down my container of food and stood up.

"I'll be right back," I told Ezger.

Iruu flitted his wings in excitement, the doughnut smell already rising from him.

I stood up and began an exaggerated, bouncing walk across the room toward the nearest faucet. As I passed the different clusters of Zhuri, more and more heads turned to stare at me. I caught a few whiffs of fear, and even one of anger—but mostly I just smelled doughnut.

I loped over to the back of a short line, wriggling my torso and hopping into the air like an eager Zhuri.

The kid in front of me turned to look back. "What are you doing, human?" he whined.

"Oh, hello!" I said to him. "I am having lunch!"

He got his drink and flitted off. I stepped up to the faucet. It was made for someone much taller and longer-armed than me, so I had to stretch out on my tiptoes to pluck a glass from the stack at the back of the sink. But I managed to get one, and the tap was close enough to fill it without too much trouble.

The dirty-gym-sock smell of the food made me want to retch, but I forced myself to smile as I turned around.

Every Zhuri in my line of sight was staring at me—a thousand compound eyes, in every direction, all glittering with light.

I took a long, bouncy step away from the faucet. The sugary doughnut smell was getting stronger, and the usual whiny-chatter racket of the cafeteria had fallen off to a murmur. They were all waiting to see what I'd do next.

I slowly raised the glass to my face and stuck my nose in it.

I'd been planning to root around with my nose like I'd seen the Zhuri do with their tubelike mouths. But I hadn't counted on just how bad the smell of the food was. I'd barely gotten my nose in there when I gagged and had to draw my whole face back, sloshing some of the food onto the floor as I did.

A little ripple of talk went through the crowd, and the smell of laughter came at me from all directions.

It was working even better than I'd imagined. I just hoped I could pull off my next move without barfing.

Don't think. Just do it.

I raised the glass to my lips, forced my lips open, poured in a mouthful—and sprayed it back out in a massive spit take.

All the Zhuri within range flitted backward to avoid the spatter as the crowd erupted in whines.

They loved it. The room was starting to smell like a doughnut factory.

I could've stopped there, and it would've been a triumph. But when the Zhuri scattered out of the way of my spit take, they'd left a wide stretch of floor open in front of me. It was empty except for a few scattered stools. My eyes landed on a stool twenty feet straight ahead. A thick cluster of Zhuri hovered in the air about five feet above it.

It was the perfect setup for a giant pratfall.

I loped forward in bouncy steps so wide that I could feel the strain in my hamstrings. My foul-smelling drink sloshed out of the cup and ran down my arm. Two steps from the empty stool, I shortened my stride, jumped onto the seat, and leaped into the air, flapping my free arm like a Zhuri's wings.

I didn't get nearly as much air as I'd hoped—I'd forgotten how much stronger gravity was on Choom—and when I fell to the floor, I landed on my hip so hard that I bounced. A shower of stinky liquid rained down on top me along with my glass, which hit me in the arm.

It would've been funnier if it had hit me in the head.

Even so, it was funny enough. The crowd was practically shrieking with delight:

"DID YOU SEE IT?"

"OH MY!"

"I DID NOT EXPECT THAT!"

I'd never smelled anything as delicious as that doughnut laughter. I got to my feet—I wanted to spring up, but my hip hurt too much from the landing, so it was more of a limp—and turned around, grinning from ear to ear. The crowd of Zhuri parted in front of me as I started back toward Ezger and Iruu.

Then my guard stepped into my field of vision, pointing his steel-pronged weapon at my chest.

He could hurt somebody with that if he's not careful, I thought.

I was still thinking it when he jabbed me just below the neck, and a couple hundred volts of electricity shot through my body.

It didn't feel good.

Oh boy, did it not feel good.

Fortunately, I passed out before the pain really sank in.

MIXED MESSAGES

THE NEXT THING I knew, I was lying on my back with a splitting headache, staring up at a beige, six-sided ceiling.

Why is everything on this planet beige and six-sided? was my first thought.

Why do I feel like I just got hit by a truck? was my second.

A Zhuri came into view, looming over my feet. I flinched at the sight of him, but he wasn't armed. Then I realized it was the principal.

"Can you understand me, Lan human?"

"Yes." My earpiece was still in my ear, and my screen was in my pocket. "I am so sorry—" I sat halfway up and immediately keeled over again from dizziness.

"It is best if you lie on the floor until the effects of the neural disrupter wear off."

No argument from me. I looked around as best I could without getting up. I was lying in the middle of what must've been his office. When I tilted my head back, I saw the guard who'd zapped me standing by the door. His weapon was still in his hands, and the sight of him gave me a jolt of fear.

"I wish to ask you, Lan human," the principal said, still standing at my feet, "what your intention was in taking the Zhuri food and jumping off the stool."

I didn't want to lie to him. But with the guard there, the truth seemed like a bad option.

"I wished to fit in," I said. "To do as the Zhuri do. I realize now that is impossible. I am sorry! I will never try it again."

The principal nodded. Then he raised his head to stare at the guard. "It is as I suspected. The human did not intend to cause smell. Your action was unnecessary and hurtful."

"The human says this now," the guard replied. "But I suspect it is not being truthful. I believe it was trying to cause the Zhuri students to make smell."

"Everyone agrees the chief educator has primary authority within this academy."

The guard rubbed his wings together. "Yes. Everyone agrees this is true."

"As chief educator, I have decided it is no longer necessary for the Executive Division to guard the human while it is inside the academy."

"My orders are to escort the human wherever it goes."

"And you may escort it to the front door, but no farther. As chief educator, I believe it is disruptive to our students for you to remain inside. Go now and wait outside the entrance. You may rejoin the human when it exits at the end of the day."

Wow. The principal was taking my side.

The guard rubbed his wings so hard that I thought they might fall off. "Everyone agrees I must report such an order to my superiors in the Executive Division," he said.

"Of course," said the principal. "You should make your report now. After all, you have nothing else to do until the end of the academic day."

The guard left, but he wasn't happy about it.

"Thank you, sir," I said.

"You are welcome," the principal told me. "I offer my deepest apologies for this accident."

I sat up again, keeping both hands flat on the floor this time to steady myself. The room felt like it was spinning.

"There is no need to stand if you do not feel healthy. You may lie here as long as necessary."

"Thank you again, sir."

I watched him walk over to the far end of the room, where there was a stool and a large screen on a horizontal, desklike platform. He sat down on the stool and began to tap at the screen.

I thought for a moment. "May I ask a question?"

"Of course."

"I know it is wrong to encourage others to make smell," I said. "But why?"

"That is a complicated question," he told me, "with many different answers. Everyone agrees that smells cause problems." He paused for a long moment, slowly rubbing his wings together. "But some people think that not all smells are equally troublesome. In fact . . . some people even think . . ."

I waited for him to finish the sentence, but he never did. He just stopped staring at me and went back to tapping at his screen.

The room was still spinning, so I closed my eyes and put my

head back down on the floor. It was throbbing with pain, but I tried to ignore it so I could think.

Finally I sat up again. "Can I ask another question?"

"Yes."

"My teacher—I mean, my learning specialist—wants me to make a presentation to our class about the human, so that my classmates can better understand us."

"I think that is an excellent idea. It would be very educational."

"I hope so! But . . . what if my presentation causes smell? Accidentally, of course. Would that be a problem?"

The principal stared at me for a while before he answered. "Everyone agrees accidents cannot be helped. As long as your presentation's purpose is educational, you should not be concerned."

"What if my presentation had some clips in it from videos that are entertaining to humans? Like, for example, television programs that cause laughter in humans?"

"What would be your purpose in showing these clips? Would it be to entertain? Or to educate?"

"To educate, sir!" I said, nodding my head for emphasis. "To show the Zhuri what kinds of things humans like to do."

"As long as your purpose is educational," he said, "I would support this. And I am sure your learning specialist would too."

I smiled in spite of the pain in my head. *I found the loophole!*

For the rest of the school day, I lay on the principal's floor, my headache and dizziness slowly fading as I dreamed up ideas for the Classroom Presentation That Might Help Save the Human Race.

Or, if the principal's armed-guard ban didn't stick, the Classroom Presentation That Might Get Me Electrocuted for Good This Time.

BY THE END of the school day, I was mostly recovered, although I was still too dizzy to walk completely straight. When I came out of the principal's office, the lobby was crowded with Zhuri kids. For the first time, I didn't smell fear coming from any of them.

Instead I smelled doughnuts.

"MAKE THE WALK!" someone yelled.

"TRY TO FLY AGAIN!" whined somebody else.

I just smiled as I weaved my way to the front door.

I was definitely on to something with this comedy business.

But that something was dangerous. When I walked outside, my guard was waiting. He usually held his prong weapon low and pointed at the ground, but as he followed me to our pod, he held the business end of it up in front of his chest, tilted slightly toward me. It was such a hostile move that as we got into the pod together, I wondered if I'd survive the trip.

Fortunately, he settled into his usual seat, and other than leaving his weapon pointed up, he ignored me. Eventually I felt safe enough to take out my screen and send a long message to Naya:

> Hi! Need HUGE FAVOR ASAP: can you search ship's archive and send me clips of best 10+ moments of physical/slapstick comedy you can think of? Scene in Ed & Fred when Ed barfs on Fred for 30 seconds straight—on Bonehedz when

175

Howie falls off balcony—also Internet vids, like basketball hoop crashing down on annoying kid's head—any others you can think of. More dumb/physical = better. Hard to explain why but VERY important. Don't send whole movies/shows, just short clips. Maybe ask other people for their favorites too?

PLEASE SEND ASAP!! NEED IT TONIGHT!! THANK YOU!!!

Ruff, ruff

After I sent the message, I jotted down some ideas on my screen for what I'd decided to call *Meet the Human!* It was going to be the funniest pro-human video presentation ever seen on any planet anywhere. It'd make every Zhuri who watched it sweat their pants—or just sweat, since they didn't wear pants—with laughter.

Once I created the video, I had to figure out how to show it to the whole planet without getting myself arrested or kicked off of Choom.

I suspected Marf could help me with that. There might even be money in it for her. So when our house came into view and Marf's pod was already parked outside, I practically jumped from my seat.

I stood at the pod door as we landed, eager to hop out as soon as it opened. Somehow I'd managed to forget all about the soldier who'd electrocuted me at lunch, even though he was still sitting just a few feet away.

As the door started to open, I heard the whine of his voice behind me.

"Everyone agrees your time is short."

I turned to look at him. He was close enough that I could see glittery shards of my face reflected back at me from his compound eyes.

"Your kind will leave here," he said. "Sooner than you think."

"Have a nice day, sir," I managed to say. Then I ran as fast as I could into the house.

I BURST INSIDE, expecting to see Marf and Ila. But the place was empty except for some open containers of Ororo food on the dining table.

"Hello? HELLLOOOOOO?"

Ila's bedroom door opened, and she sprang into the room. Marf lumbered in after her, carrying a bag of tools.

"Hi! How was school?" Ila practically skipped over to the food at the table.

"What were you doing in the bedroom?"

"Nothing. Marf just wanted to see it." She popped a chunk of purple Ororo food into her mouth.

Something weird was definitely going on. Marf moved past me, headed for the door with her bag.

"Can I talk to you about something important?" I asked.

"I am in a great hurry," she said. "But I have something I want to give you. Can you walk with me to my pod?"

"Sure thing." I followed her outside, past the guards in front of our door. "Why are you in such a rush?"

"Because sometimes events move faster than we'd like."

"What events?"

"STOP! THE HUMAN CANNOT BOARD THAT POD WITHOUT APPROVAL!" The guards were flitting toward us, their weapons out.

"The human is not going anywhere," Marf informed them. Then she turned back to me. "Wait here a moment." She disappeared inside her pod for a few seconds. When she came out, she was holding the two-foot-tall Krik robot she'd shown us the night before. She handed it to me.

"I want you to have this."

"Why?" I stared up into her big dark eyes—and, for the first time, I saw the sadness that Ezger had told me about.

"Because if we don't see each other again, I'd like you to have something that helps you remember me."

A clammy feeling started to creep through my whole body. "What are you talking about? Why wouldn't we see each other again?"

Instead of answering, Marf gestured toward the little robot in my hands. "The power switch is behind its neck. Don't leave it on, or it'll eat all your electronics." She turned away, toward the pod door.

"Wait! Marf! You're freaking me out here!"

"Goodbye, Lan. I enjoy your company! But I must go."

"*Wait!* Where are you—"

She shut the door before I could finish the sentence. Two seconds later, the pod shot straight up in the air like a silent rocket. It crossed the fence with a piercing *BZZZT!*, paused in midair, then zipped off toward the center of the city.

I looked down at the silver metal Krik. Its lifeless eyes stared back at me. The creeping dread was getting worse. I went back into the house.

Ila was at the table, eating Ororo food and drumming her fingers to a song in her head. "What the heck is going on?" I asked her.

"Nothing. What's up with you?" she said through a mouthful.

"Where was Marf going? And why were you in the bedroom together?"

"She just wanted to see it. What do you think—we were making out?"

Just then, my screen beeped with a message from Mom:

What happened at school today????

I knocked out a quick reply:

Long story. Can explain when you're home.
But good news!

Then I went back to grilling my sister. "Ila—*what's going on*? Tell me!"

She snorted. "Nothing! Why are you being so paranoid?"

My screen beeped again. When I looked down at Mom's reply, my stomach dropped to somewhere around my knees:

It's not good. Turn on the TV.

19

THE DOOR IN THE FLOOR

I RAN TO the couch and turned on the TV news. It was showing a segment about some kind of hive construction project the Unified Government had just announced.

"What's happening?" Ila asked.

"I don't know yet. Just wait."

We didn't have to wait long. The next segment began with a shot of my school.

"Today marked a disturbing new development in the Unified Government's human immigration experiment. The children of the Iseeyii Interspecies Academy were terrorized during their midday nutrition when a human younger ran amok."

There must have been a drone camera somewhere in the lunchroom, because the image switched to a grainy, slow-motion replay of my leap onto the empty stool. The lower legs of one of the Zhuri kids in the cluster above me were just visible, and in slow motion, the way I flapped my free hand in the air made it look like I was reaching up to grab at the kid's leg.

Even worse, with the sound stretched out, the delighted

shrieks of all the kids in the lunchroom sounded more like cries of agony.

"Without warning, the violent and primitive animal lunged at a defenseless Zhuri child, attempting to drag it to the floor."

"THAT'S NOT WHAT HAPPENED!" I yelled at the screen. My dread was curdling into panic.

"Iseeyii's chief educator expressed shock and concern at this act of violence."

The image switched to an interview with the principal outside the school's front door.

"This was both unnecessary and hurtful," the principal said. "For the safety of all our students, I have taken steps to change our security arrangements by—"

His interview ended in mid-sentence, the image replaced by an old Earth horror-movie clip of a man with knives for fingers chasing a screaming teenager.

"It is unknown at this time whether the new security measures will include banning the human animals from attending school."

"THAT'S NOT WHAT HE SAID! HE WAS TALKING ABOUT THE GUARD!"

"Regardless, the human presence on Choom may come to an end as early as tomorrow."

The image switched again, to a shot of a cluster of older Zhuri, led by the dead-eyed chief servant, flitting from a pod into a building.

"In response to the latest violence, the chief servant has scheduled an emergency meeting with representatives from the Immigration Division. The meeting will take place in the late morning, after which everyone agrees the Unified Government would be foolish not to announce the end of the human experiment."

Ila stared at me in horror. "*What* did you do?"

My whole body felt like it had turned to jelly. All I could do was shake my head. "I just made them laugh."

"YOU'VE GOT TO understand," I told my parents for the third time, "they all *loved* it. And the principal was totally on my side! He practically *told* me to make a video! With *comedy* in it! That whole news report was a lie!"

"I know," said Mom as she rubbed some of Hunf's antivenom cream onto her arm. "Unfortunately, it was an effective lie."

By the time Mom and Dad had left work, huge antihuman protests were underway outside both their workplaces, and Mom had gotten hit with a stream of venom. The TV news had claimed the protests were more evidence that we were causing disagreement, even though what had really caused the protests was the TV news's lying about what I did in the lunchroom.

They were still running the lie on the news every few minutes, and the longer they kept it up, the worse the protests got. Judging by the noise of the whining we could hear as we sat at our dining table, there were at least a thousand angry Zhuri outside our subdivision.

"I'm sorry." Tears welled up in my eyes. "This is all my fault."

Mom reached across the table to take my hand. "It's not your fault. You won over a whole school full of kids. That's *good*. And not everybody believes the news. Leeni's on our side, and I get

182

the sense he's not the only one. There are a lot of people in the Immigration Division who I think want to give us a chance."

"The trouble is," Dad said, "will they have the courage to speak up for us in that meeting tomorrow? Or will 'everyone agree' we should leave?"

"I don't know," Mom admitted. "I can't tell how much influence Immigration has inside the government. It seems like the Executive Division's the real center of power."

"The Executive's run by that old guy who came to dinner, right?" Ila asked. "The one with the dead spots in his eyes? Who said art was poison?"

Mom and Dad both nodded.

"And at this meeting tomorrow," Ila went on, "he's going to decide whether we stay or go?"

"Unfortunately, that's what it sounds like," Dad said.

My screen beeped. It was a message from Naya.

> These are the best clips I could find. WHY DO YOU WANT THEM?? So random!!
>
> Ruff, ruff

Attached to the message were a dozen files. "Naya just sent me the clips," I announced. I'd already explained my idea for *Meet the Human!* Mom and Dad had both agreed it was worth a shot.

"Get to work on the video," Mom told me. "Your father and I will try to figure out how we can get the Zhuri public to watch it. It's going to be risky, and there isn't much time. But Leeni might be willing to help us."

"I'll try to find Marf before school and ask her too," I said.

Mom and Dad gave me quizzical looks. "How can Marf help?"

"I don't know for sure. She won't give me a straight answer to anything. But yesterday . . ." I paused. "She made me swear I wouldn't tell you this. But she's got some kind of illegal business. She offered me a ton of money for my *Birdleys* videos. At first I thought she was reselling them to other Ororo. But now that I think about it, she might have wanted to sell them to Zhuri instead. Maybe she can help us distribute a video to people."

"How much money did she offer you?" Ila asked.

"I think it was four hundred rhee an episode?"

"That's it?"

"What do you mean, 'that's it?' "

Ila bit her lip. "She gave me five thousand."

"What?"

Ila reached into her pocket and pulled out a shiny metallic disc, crosshatched with circuitry. She showed it to us in the palm of her hand. "Supposedly, there's a ton of money on this chip. Unless Marf lied to me."

Mom was shocked. We all were. "Why did Marf give you five thousand rhee?"

"So I'd play a song for her." Ila stood up. "There's something I have to show you guys."

ILA LED US into her bedroom. "I'm sorry I didn't tell you right away. I just didn't want to mess it up." She opened one of the bottom drawers along the wall. It was empty, but she bent down and probed with her fingers along the inside of the upper frame.

"Oh geez, where is it . . . ? Here!" She pressed an unseen

button. A few feet away, a three-foot-square trapdoor opened in the floor.

"What the heck?" Dad exclaimed.

Ila reached into the secret compartment and pulled out an acoustic guitar. The body was made from some kind of red plastic, and it was strung with gold wire.

She took the guitar over to the bed and sat down, laying it across her lap. Her face practically glowed with joy. I hadn't seen that kind of look from Ila since we'd left Earth. It was like she'd suddenly rediscovered her whole reason for living.

"It took forever to tune," she said as she strummed the guitar lovingly. "And Marf had to rebuild the bridge a couple of times. But it sounds *so* good now. I played 'World Turning Round' for her, and she recorded it on one of those drone cameras. Then she built me this compartment to hide the guitar in. She said I could keep it as long as I didn't tell anybody."

"How long was she here?" I asked.

"A few hours. She came in the middle of the day."

So that was where Marf had gone when she left the lunchroom.

"This is amazing," said Mom, shaking her head.

Dad nodded. "And it explains something . . . I think."

"What?"

"This afternoon at work," he said, "one of the Zhuri supervisors came up to me. He was whispering, like he didn't want anyone to hear him. He said, 'Can you make the noises?' When I said, 'What noises?' he got spooked and walked away. I think he must've been talking about music. But this would've been before Marf recorded you today."

"She already had my *Pop Singer* videos," Ila told him. "She got them off my screen when she stole it from Lan. That's why I played 'World Turning Round' for her—when she gave me the guitar, I started to play 'Under a Blue Sky,' but she said she already had that one."

"I bet she'd already sold the *Pop Singer* clips to people," Dad said. "And the guy at work saw one of them. For him to approach me like that . . . he must've really loved it."

Mom looked at me. "Can you get hold of Marf? Right now?"

I shook my head. "I don't know how to get in touch with her. I either see her at school, or she comes here." I turned to Ila. "What about you? Can you reach her?"

It was Ila's turn to shake her head. "She said she'd come find me when she wanted to make another video."

"Does anybody remember how to get to their house?" Mom asked.

"It was all a blur," said Dad. "We were moving too fast. And on the way home, it was too dark to see."

"The guards outside might know." Mom turned and started for the door. "I'll tell them we need more antivenom cream from Marf's parents. Maybe they'll give us a ride."

Unsurprisingly, the guards wouldn't give us a ride. They also wouldn't answer Mom's questions about how to get to Marf's house, or even how to get in touch with Leeni to ask him for help.

"Leeni's planning to come by in the morning," Mom told us. "Until then, I don't know what we can do."

"I can try to find Marf before school," I offered.

"That doesn't leave us much time. The government's having their meeting in the morning." Mom sighed. "But I guess it's all we can do." She turned to me. "Get to work on that video."

"Clips of people tripping over themselves aren't going to save us," Ila told me. "You should make a video with music instead of comedy in it."

"No," said Mom. "We should make one with both."

THE FOUR OF us worked on it together, huddled over my screen at the dining table until the middle of the night. When we finished, *Meet the Human!* was ninety seconds of physical-comedy gold, followed by Ila's tear-jerking version of "Under a Blue Sky" from the *Pop Singer* show. The song didn't have anything to do with the comedy, but somehow it all seemed to work.

"Are you sure we shouldn't use a different song?" Ila asked. "I mean, if people have already seen this one—"

Dad interrupted her. "Sweetheart, if the whole planet had heard 'Blue Sky' already, they wouldn't be having a meeting to talk about throwing us out. They'd be breaking our door down with free guitars."

Or throwing us in jail, I thought. But I didn't say it out loud.

"Trust us, honey," Mom told Ila. "You want to play the hit."

"It's good, right?" I asked. "It's a good video?"

"It's better than good," Mom said. "We just have to get it in front of people without the government censoring it. But there's nothing we can do until morning. Let's get some sleep."

As stirred up as I was, it had been an exhausting day, and the auto-massaging mattress worked its magic. Within minutes, I was dead asleep.

An hour before dawn, I woke up to the screams of Zhuri soldiers pointing electrified prongs at my face.

EVERYONE AGREES
(EXCEPT WHEN THEY DON'T)

"YEEEHHHHEEEE!"

"REEEEHHHEEEEE!"

"HEEREEYEEEHEEE!"

They were shrieking at the top of their lungs, but I couldn't understand a word. My earpiece and screen were lying next to the bed. When I reached for them, one of the soldiers stuck his prong so close to my ear that I felt the hair on the side of my head rise up.

"Sorry!" I raised my hands in the air.

They gestured with their prongs. *Get out of bed.*

I did. They screamed at me again.

"I don't understand you! Can I please just—" My hand trembling with fear, I motioned toward my screen a second time. This time, all three of them stuck their prongs in my face.

"Please! It's to talk! To understand you!"

They either didn't get it or didn't care. Instead they motioned for me to leave the room. I did as I was told.

The rest of my family was already in the living room, getting shrieked at by more soldiers. There were a dozen of them, all pointing their pronged weapons at us. One was clearly in charge, because whenever he started yelling, the others stopped.

Mom was trying to reason with them. Dad had his arm around Ila, trying to comfort her. I just tried to stand still and hope nobody electrocuted me.

The leader assigned one soldier to guard each of us, then sent the others to search our rooms. As we heard them yanking open drawers, the leader focused his yelling on Mom.

She kept shaking her head. "Please. I don't understand. . . . I need my screen. . . . Please."

The leader eventually figured out that if he wanted any information, he'd have to let Mom use her translator. Once he did, we were able to follow her half of the conversation.

"Please tell us how we can help you." Even when she was getting threatened with electrocution, Mom didn't drop her *see how peace-loving and reasonable I am?* tone. "We wish to be of service. . . . Yes. . . . We did not know that was illegal. . . . Of course we will cooperate."

She turned to Ila, who'd only just managed to stop crying. "Sweetheart, they want the guitar."

Ila let out a wail. The leader shrieked at her.

"We don't have a choice," Mom said. "They know it's here. They've seen the video you recorded for Marf yesterday."

While Ila cried on the couch, Dad went to her room and showed the soldiers where the guitar was. One of them carried it past us and out the door to a waiting pod.

After that, things got a little more calm, but no less scary. The soldiers brought all of our screens to the dining table and started poking at them, presumably looking for videos even though they couldn't make heads or tails of our human-language interfaces. Meanwhile, the leader kept questioning Mom.

"We didn't know it was wrong," she said. "We are so sorry. . . . We are so very sorry. We didn't know. . . . She is a school friend of my youngest child. . . . She took the screen without permission. When she returned it, we did not know she had copied anything. . . . They gave us food and medicine. . . . We never would have done it, but no one told us it was wrong. . . . It is not frowned upon on our planet. . . . No. We never took it out of the house. . . ."

It sounded to me like the interrogation was going okay, but I was wrong. After a while, two of the soldiers stepped out of the house and returned with four sets of the toaster oven–sized handcuffs I'd seen them use on Dad after the venom attack. They trussed our hands up in them, gathered all our screens, and led us outside, where three pods were waiting.

The whole time, we'd been hearing the chants of protestors in the distance. But until we walked onto the lawn, I hadn't realized just how many of them there were. When we appeared, a swarm of thousands rose up at the edge of the subdivision and spread across the electric fence almost the whole distance to our house. The air stank of gasoline anger, and the protestors were so riled up that the fence buzzed constantly as they slammed into it and got zapped.

We were halfway to the pod that would take us who knows where when the swarm suddenly scattered as the protestors flew out of the way of an incoming pod. It passed through the fence with an electric thunderclap and landed just a few feet away, heat billowing from its engine.

A stream of armed Zhuri spilled through its door, shrieking as they ran toward us with their prong weapons extended.

I shut my eyes and prayed it wouldn't hurt too much.

But they weren't coming for us. Their targets were the Zhuri soldiers who'd arrested us. The two groups faced off, a dozen on each side, shrieking at each other and whipping their wings every which way as the buzzing blue flicker of the fence lit them up and the swarm screamed overhead. A strong undercurrent of sour-milk fear began to mix with the gasoline anger.

The whole situation was as confusing as it was terrifying— and when I realized the person in charge of the soldiers who'd shown up to help us was Leeni, I got even more confused.

"What's happening?" I yelled at Dad, who was closest to me.

"I don't know!" he yelled back.

Mom was too far away to hear me over the noise, and I was worried if I took a step without permission, I'd get zapped. So I just stood there, helpless in my toaster-oven handcuffs, watching the tennis match of shrieking. It went on until it must have occurred to the Zhuri that it'd be much easier to argue inside, where there wasn't a swarm of protestors screaming over their heads.

They marched us back into the house, and the argument quickly narrowed down to just Leeni and the leader of the group that was trying to haul us away.

As they bickered back and forth, and all two-dozen-plus Zhuri rubbed their wings together in agony over the disagreement, Mom—who was still the only one of us with a translator— explained what was happening.

"The soldiers who want to take us away are from the

Executive Division," she said. "They're the ones who've been guarding our house and escorting us around the whole time. The new soldiers—the ones who just showed up with Leeni—are from the Immigration Division. Leeni's claiming the Executive soldiers don't have the right to arrest us. He says that as long as we're inside the house, only Immigration has that authority."

Eventually Leeni and the Immigration soldiers won the argument. The Executive soldiers took our handcuffs off and gave us back our screens, but they took the spare screens and Ila's guitar with them when they left.

"What happened?" I asked when I finally got my earpiece back in and could understand what Leeni was saying.

"The Ororo student has been selling your Earth videos illegally," Leeni explained. "The ones that show Ila making sound with the machine have caused great emotion."

Even though we'd already guessed that was what Marf had been up to, we all pretended to look shocked. "Is it a bad thing to cause such emotion?" Dad asked.

Leeni stared at him for a long moment. "Everyone agrees that emotions cause problems. But some people think not *all* emotions do so. Some people even think . . ."

Then he stopped talking, just like the principal had done.

"What do some people think?" Mom prompted him.

Leeni rubbed his wings together. "Some people think there are positive emotions. And those should be encouraged."

"Does music cause positive emotions?"

"Some people think so."

"What about laughter?" I asked.

Leeni looked at me. "Some people think that is also positive."

He rubbed his wings again. "But everyone agrees the Executive Division does not think this way. The Executive believes these videos with music are a threat to the planet's peace. Their security forces are trying to find the Ororo younger and stop her from spreading the videos. They came here tonight looking for evidence. They also wished to take you to the spaceport for immediate removal from the planet."

My stomach dropped.

"Can they do that?" Mom asked.

"Everyone agrees now that they do not have this authority. But they have gone to request an order from the chief servant that would allow them to remove you. I believe they will return with this order in a short time."

"What about the meeting this morning? The one to discuss our case?"

"It will likely be canceled," said Leeni, "because it no longer matters. The chief servant will almost certainly order your removal. You will be placed on a shuttle and returned to the human ship immediately."

"Leeni." Mom walked over to stand in front of him. "If they send us back to the ship, the human species will perish."

"I understand this," said Leeni. "There are some who wish it was not the case."

"Those who wish for us to survive—what do they suggest we do?"

Leeni rubbed his wings together. "It is difficult. In order for you to stay, everyone would have to agree that you should. But at the moment, everyone agrees the opposite."

"If the Zhuri people could see the videos—the ones that

cause positive emotions—would they be more likely to agree the human should stay?" Mom asked.

"Some people think so," said Leeni. "This is why the Executive Division has moved so quickly to stop the musical videos from spreading."

"How can we help to spread them?"

The question was too much for Leeni. His head snapped back like he'd been smacked, and his fear smell filled the room.

"I am a senior official of the Unified Government," he said. "I cannot encourage activities that are illegal. If I knew of such videos, I would have to destroy them."

For a long time, nobody said anything.

Then I had an idea. "What if the videos were educational?"

Leeni turned his head to me. "Everyone agrees that if something is educational, it is appropriate. But the place for education is school."

I looked out the window. The sky was beginning to turn the blue-green color of a Choom dawn. "Can I go to school today?" I asked.

"The Executive Division is responsible for escorting human youngers to school," Leeni said. "I am sure they will no longer do so. When they return, they will take all four of you to the spaceport for immediate removal."

My shoulders slumped, and I heard Mom let out a frustrated sigh.

Leeni lowered his head and rubbed his wings together slowly, like he was agonizing over something. Finally he spoke.

"But if you wish to go to school early," he said, "I could escort you now."

194

PUT YOUR HEADS
IN THE AIR

WHATEVER WEIRD LEGAL loophole Leeni was using to take Ila and me to school, it didn't apply to Mom and Dad. They hugged us goodbye just inside the front door.

"I should stay with you guys," said Ila.

"No, you shouldn't," Mom told her. "Stick with Lan. Don't let each other out of your sight. Message us if anything happens. We'll do the same."

"What are you and Dad going to do?" I asked.

"We'll stay here for the moment. And try to think of ways we can be helpful." Mom gave Ila and me each another hug. "Now get out of here while you still can."

"Don't leave without us," I said. I was trying to make a joke, but Mom and Dad didn't take it that way.

"Do everything you can to stay on the planet," Dad said. "Don't worry about us."

"Be peaceful and kind, but don't go quietly," Mom added. "This isn't just about us. If we leave Choom, they'll never let another human back in."

There were still half a dozen Executive Division soldiers outside, but there were twice as many from the Immigration Division. The ones from Immigration escorted us to Leeni's pod as the Executives screamed in anger along with the crowd of protestors swarming the fence over our heads.

We got in the pod with Leeni and a pair of Immigration soldiers. Within seconds we were in the air. When we crossed the fence, the protestors scattered out of our way. After we passed, a few dozen of them regrouped and tried to follow us. Fortunately, that was about as effective as humans trying to run down a car on the highway, and they quickly dropped out of sight.

For the rest of the trip, the city below us was quiet and empty. Only a few scattered pods dotted the early morning sky.

"Is our school open this early?" I asked Leeni.

"Ordinarily, it is not," he answered. "But I have contacted the chief educator and asked him to meet you there."

"Do you know the chief educator?" I asked.

"It is better if we do not discuss our relationship," Leeni said.

Ila switched off her translator. "Do you understand what's up with Leeni?" she asked me.

I switched mine off too. "I think so. He's trying to help us. But he can't help us *too* much, or he'll get in trouble."

"So, what? He's going to claim he 'accidentally' flew us to school?" Ila shook her head. "Good luck with *that.*"

It was so early when we landed at the academy that there weren't any protestors out front. Nobody else was around either. When Leeni walked us up to the front door and pressed an entry button, it took a few minutes for a Krik custodian to open the door and poke his head out.

"School's closed!" he growled.

"The humans have an early meeting with the chief educator," said Leeni.

He looked us up and down, then shrugged. "You can wait in the hallway. Don't smudge the floor! It's clean."

Leeni left us at the door, and we went inside to sit against the wall in front of the principal's office. Other than an occasional custodian pushing a cleaning machine past us, the building was empty. Its high-ceilinged lobby felt much bigger without crowds of Zhuri and Krik students moving through it.

"I'm starving," Ila said. Even at a near whisper, her voice echoed to the ceiling. "Aren't you?"

"I wasn't until you mentioned it."

We sat there for what must've been an hour until the principal showed up.

"I was surprised to hear you were coming," he told us. "When I saw the news reports, I did not expect the government to allow you to return to school."

"The news reports aren't telling the truth about us," I said.

"They do not seem to be telling the truth about me either. Come into my office."

HE SAT ON the stool behind his desk-sized screen. We parked ourselves on a bench across from him. It was made for Zhuri adults, and so high that our legs dangled off the floor.

"The official from the Immigration Division said you had educational material you wished to share with me. What kind of material is it?"

"It's a video," I said. "Do you want to watch it?"

"Of course. I am an educator."

Marf's transmitter worked on the principal's screen the same way it worked on our TV back at the house. I cast *Meet the Human!* onto his screen. The video began with a close-up of my face, smiling into the camera. I could barely hear my original words under the *yeeheeeeheeee* of the Zhuri translation that played over them:

"Hi! I'm Lan Mifune, and I'd like to clear up some misunderstandings about the human species. We're not violent! But we *are* clumsy. Very, very clumsy . . ."

The first minute of the video was a compilation of humans tripping over things, falling down stairs, and getting conked on the head. As the principal watched it, I took deep breaths in through my nose, hoping to smell a reaction from him. There was nothing, and I started to worry the video wasn't as funny as I'd thought it was.

But then we got to the barfing scene from *Ed and Fred.*

"Humans don't spit venom on each other," my voiceover explained, "but sometimes we *do* get a little sick to our stomachs. . . ."

Ed and Fred was one of the funniest shows of all time, and the barfing scene was the best moment in the whole series. Ed discovered a new soft drink that he thought was delicious, but it made his stomach upset. Even so, he loved the taste so much that he couldn't stop drinking it. He bought a whole case, downed it in one sitting, and then barfed it all out on Fred while they were stuck in the back of a moving car.

What made the scene so funny was that the barf just kept

going, and going, and going . . . It went on forever, way past the point where you'd think *This can't possibly last any longer.* The first time I saw the episode, it made me laugh so hard that my face hurt. Even rewatching it for the twentieth time, I couldn't help giggling.

It worked on the principal too. The doughnut odor wafted over to us. Ila turned to me with a big grin on her face. I smiled back at her.

Then the barf scene ended, and the music segment began.

"And when humans are feeling down, there's nothing that picks us up like the sound of music. . . ."

Ila appeared, spotlit on the *Pop Singer* stage as she strummed the opening chords of "Under a Blue Sky."

> *Well, the nights have been black*
> *And the days have been gray*
> *I can't find what I lost*
> *When my hope went away*

This time, I saw the principal react before I smelled him. He sat up straight on his stool, his head swaying to the right . . . and then to the left . . . and then back again, all in time with the music. When the scent hit me, it was sweet and sharp at the same time, like honeysuckle mixed with mint.

As Ila and I watched him, our eyes widening in surprise, his whole body began to sway, shifting direction with every down-beat. As the song swelled to its anthem-like chorus, his wings started to flutter, and he rose up several inches off his seat.

I want to live under a blue sky
Don't want to numb the pain just to get by
I want to give living a new try
Gonna find a way to wash the rain from my eyes

He hovered in the air, his body swaying in snakelike curves as the room filled with the scent of honeysuckle and mint. When the song ended, he slowly sank back onto his stool, then shook his head softly like he was coming out of a trance.

I looked at Ila. Her mouth was hanging open in shock. So was mine.

"That was very educational," he told us. "I wish to show it to the entire academy."

"Can we do it quickly, sir?" I asked him. "Because I don't think we have much time."

AN HOUR LATER, Ila and I stood with the principal in front of a giant screen on the wall above the faucets in the lunchroom. The entire school was facing us. The shorter Krik stood in the front, with the Zhuri covering every available bit of space behind and above them. From where we were standing, it looked like a solid wall of kids looming in front of us.

Marf wasn't there. Neither was Ezger. According to a news report we'd watched on the principal's screen while waiting for school to begin, they were wanted by the government for "distributing emotional content that threatens Choom's peace." The report warned its viewers to "avoid all contact with this dangerous and highly emotional material," and it asked anyone who saw Marf or Ezger to inform the Executive Division immediately.

I was terrified for my friends, and watching the report with the principal, I'd started to worry that he might turn us in. But instead he'd shut off the TV without a word. Now he was getting ready to show some "dangerous and highly emotional material" to a couple thousand kids. If he was afraid the whole Unified Government was about to come down on his head, he didn't show it.

Judging by the doughnut smell, the Zhuri kids were already primed to like what they saw. As we stood waiting for the video to start, the ones in front whined requests at me:

"Do the walk!"

"Try to fly!"

"Fall down again!"

Ila gave me a bewildered look. "What did you *do* yesterday?"

I shrugged. "Mostly I just tripped over stuff. They're easy laughs."

The principal took flight, zooming up to hover over our heads. "Quiet, please, children!" he shrieked, and they all obeyed instantly—a second later, the only sound in the room was the steady *thrummm* of hovering wings.

"The human youngers," he told the crowd, "have been kind enough to create an educational video for us, so that we may better understand their species. Please direct your attention to the screen."

He dropped back to the floor as a mechanical shade extended over the skylight, covering the room in semidarkness.

Then the video began to play. It was a hit from the opening

seconds—with every pratfall, another wave of fresh-baked dough-nut rose up from the crowd. When we got to the barfing scene, the smell grew twice as thick, and the chitters of excitement from the Zhuri kids almost drowned out the soundtrack.

Then Ila appeared on the screen, two stories tall, and began to sing "Under a Blue Sky."

What happened next took my breath away. As the doughnut smell faded, replaced by honeysuckle and mint, the whole crowd of Zhuri began to sway back and forth in time with the music, the same way the principal had. But instead of just one person's body tracing an S-curve in midair, there were two thousand—and all of them were in perfect sync.

The whole school full of Zhuri danced as one, in a wall of movement that looked as peaceful as it was powerful. Beneath them, the Krik in front bounced on their feet and bobbed their heads. Unlike the Zhuri, they weren't quite in sync, and their bod-ies created a ragged green line of movement under the Zhuri's massive wave of energy.

It was so beautiful that I got a lump in my throat. When I looked over at Ila, she was crying. I think if it were physically possible for them to cry, the Zhuri would have too. Watching them dance was so hypnotic, and I'd had so little sleep over the past days, that as the song went on, I started to get light-headed.

Then, just before the final chorus, the music stopped and the screen went dark.

The spell it had cast over the crowd broke, and the positive energy drained away, leaving only the *thrummm* of the Zhuri's beating wings as everyone looked at each other in confusion and disappointment.

What just happened?

A commotion rose up at the back, by the entrance doors—whining, jostling, some kind of disturbance. We tried to peer through the mass of people, but it was too thick, and the light was too low, for us to see what was happening. We could hear the disruption moving through the room toward us, but it wasn't until the line of Krik broke open right in front of us that we saw the soldiers.

I don't know how many of them there were. I only saw the first wedge, needles of blue light arcing across their prong weapons as they rushed at us.

They zapped the principal first. Ila and I were next.

It didn't hurt as much as it had the day before. Or maybe I just passed out faster.

THE KIND OF TROUBLE
YOU DON'T GET OUT OF

MY HEADACHE WAS bad. But not as bad as the fact that I was trapped in a coffin.

At least it felt like a coffin. It must've been built for a Zhuri, because I was squeezed into it so tight that I couldn't move my head or take a full breath. My back and chest were pressed between the top and bottom walls like a dead bug in a display case. I could move my arms and legs sideways, but only for a few inches until they hit the walls on either side.

My head was turned to the left, and there was just enough light to see the wall in front of me. It was smooth plastic, in the same stupid color of beige as everything else on Choom.

I could hear shrieking in the distance. It sounded like protestors. But someone had taken away my screen and earpiece, so I didn't know for sure.

I lay there for a while. I don't know how long. Thirty minutes? An hour? It was hard to judge time.

There was a faint rumbling noise, like machinery starting up. The walls trembled.

My coffin was moving.

I felt my equilibrium change. Was I tilting down? Up? I was still so dizzy from the neural disrupter that I couldn't tell.

The walls above and below me started to expand. I had just enough time to wonder if I was about to fall before I did.

"AAGH!"

I landed in a heap on a spongy floor. I was in a small beige room with no doors or windows. The opening I'd fallen from in the ceiling had already vanished. The room was empty except for a pair of stools and a table.

My screen and earpiece were on the table.

I tried to get up, but I was too dizzy to walk. So I half crawled, half dragged myself over to the table. I put the earpiece in and took my screen, laying it sideways on the floor in front of my head so I could look at it without sitting up.

There was a message from Mom, almost an hour old:

Troops arriving don't come home

I dragged myself over to the side wall so I could sit up and prop myself against it. I sent messages to Mom, Dad, and Ila:

Where are you? I think I am in jail

Nobody answered. I figured as much.

The headache was killing me. Not literally. At least I didn't think so. But wow, did it hurt.

I decided I should try to get up. I had no idea what was happening, but I felt like being able to stand would be a plus.

With my back against the wall, I pushed myself up onto my feet. Then I took a step forward so I was standing free. Right away I started to careen to one side.

Too soon. I lurched back against the wall and slid down onto my butt.

A couple minutes later, I tried again. This time I lasted a little longer before I had to plop back down.

I'd just stood up for the third time when a door appeared in the wall and a Zhuri entered. The door closed behind him, leaving no trace of where it had been.

The Zhuri motioned to one of the two stools. "Sit."

It was only about four steps over to the stool. But that was two more than I could manage. After the second step, I felt myself listing to one side. I overcorrected, lost my feet, and came crashing down on top of the stool.

It must've looked hilarious. But I didn't get any doughnut smell from the Zhuri. He just stared down at me as I wobbled onto my knees, righted the stool, and somehow managed to dump myself on top of it.

I had to grab hold of the table with both hands so I wouldn't keel over.

"Human Lan Mifune, who have you conspired with?"

"Do you have any headache medicine, sir?"

"I ask the questions."

Uh-oh. Gasoline. He's mad.

"You are part of a plot to disrupt Choom's peace. Who has assisted you in this?"

"There's no plot, sir," I said. "We want peace too."

"Who told you to create the emotional content?"

"Nobody did, sir. We just thought people would like—that it would be educational for them."

"Did Senior Official Leeni conspire with you?"

"No, sir."

"Did Chief Educator Hiyew conspire with you?"

"No, sir. We didn't conspire. He just thought it was educational too."

The interrogator's head snapped back. The gasoline smell got worse.

"Human Lan Mifune. Listen closely. What do you hear?"

"Protestors?" The chanting had been going on ever since I woke up, but after so many days of hearing them in the distance, I'd mostly stopped noticing.

"Those are Zhuri citizens, poisoned with the sickness of emotion," he said. "They have great anger, and you are the cause of it. If you continue to tell me lies, I will send you out among the swarm—and they will destroy you."

This is really not going well.

"I'm telling you the truth, sir."

"Who among the Zhuri conspired with you?"

"Nobody!"

"Lies!"

He was getting so angry that he was giving off a whole new smell. It was a harsh, chemical stink, like menthol and rubbing alcohol.

"We know there is a conspiracy against the Unified Government. You will tell us who is responsible—" He paused, his head drawing back again. "Are you making smell at me?"

"Humans don't make smell, sir."

The menthol-alcohol stink was getting much stronger, and I realized it wasn't coming from him after all. He leaned in toward me, his tubelike mouth twitching rapidly. Then he stood up, raising his head and slowly turning it as he inspected the seams where the ceiling met the wall. He walked toward the far corner, his head still raised and his mouth twitching.

He must've been searching for the source of the stink. It was so strong now that it felt like it was searing my nostrils. I tried not to breathe through my nose.

The interrogator flitted up into the air, raising his face to inspect the seam between the ceiling and wall. There must've been some kind of air duct up there.

I watched him slowly fly along the wall, his upturned mouth following the edge of the ceiling.

Then his wings stopped flitting.

He dropped out of the air, crashing in a heap on the floor. His collapse shocked me so much that I jumped up from my stool and almost fell over myself. I hoped my dizziness was from the neural disrupter's side effects and not whatever had just knocked out my interrogator.

Leaning against the wall for support, I made my way over to where I thought the door had been. I knocked hard on it. Whatever had just happened to the interrogator, I didn't want to get blamed.

"Hello? HELLO? HELLOOOO!"

There was no answer. Still leaning on the wall, I made my way over to the interrogator's crumpled body. He didn't look like he was breathing. Then again, I wasn't exactly an expert on Zhuri biology.

I went back to the door and pounded on it again, turning up the volume on my screen's speaker and directing it at the door so the translation would broadcast as far as possible.

"HELLOOOO! HELLLOOOOO? SOMEBODY PLEASE HELP!"

I didn't hear anything except the distant, angry chants of protestors outside the building. My chest started to tighten with panic. I was right on the edge of a meltdown when the door opened.

Marf filled the doorway, the strap from a thick satchel across her chest.

"MRRRRMMMM . . . !"

The sound of her sexy-actress rasp in my earpiece was so comforting that my panicky fear started to loosen its grip on my chest. "Oh good!" she said. "You still have your translator. Come help me find your sister."

I fell into her arms, and she gave me a quick, warm hug. Then she grabbed my upper arms with both hands and stood me up straight.

"I am glad to see you too. But there is no time for affection."

"I wasn't trying to hug you," I said. "I'm just not real good at walking right now."

"Oh. That could be a problem. Try to hang on to the wall."

She stepped away from the door. I grabbed the wall with one hand and did my best to follow. Beyond her was some kind of control room, with stools set up in front of an array of screens and panels.

Four Zhuri were crumpled on the floor next to their stools.

"What did you *do* to them?"

"It's a long story. I'm very clever. Hurry up."

Marf was headed for a door a few feet from the one I'd just exited. I lurched after her, grabbing the edge of the control panel for support.

Marf opened the narrow door, turned herself sideways, and squeezed her body through the opening. I got as far as the doorway, which led into a second interrogation room. Nobody was inside it except Marf. She picked up a human earpiece and screen from the table, then motioned for me to get out of the way so she could squeeze back through the doorway.

She handed the screen and earpiece to me. "These must be your sister's. I think she's in the main detention area. Put them in your pocket and hold on to my arm."

I let her half drag me past the Zhuri bodies on the floor toward a larger door on the far wall.

"We have to hurry," she told me. "It won't be long before they wake up."

I glanced back at the bodies. "They're not all dead?"

"Of course not! I'm trying *very* hard not to commit any crimes that can't be forgiven once we overthrow the government."

"We're *overthrowing the government?*" She hauled me through the door into a long hallway, empty except for a couple of unconscious Zhuri lying on the floor.

"I'm afraid it's my only choice," she said as she lugged me down the hall. "I seem to have gotten myself in the kind of trouble you don't get out of unless you change the rules of the game."

She paused at a door, checking the Zhuri-language sign on it before moving on. "It'll be quite good for you, I think—a new government will almost certainly welcome humans. That is, if we can stop the current one from killing all of you in a desperate attempt to hang on to power—aah! Here we are!"

She stopped at another door and examined the locking mechanism in the wall next to it. "Hmm. Biometrics . . . Lean against the wall, will you? I need both hands free."

I did as I was told. Marf lumbered down the hallway toward the nearest unconscious Zhuri.

"Personally, I'd rather *not* overthrow the government," she said over her shoulder. "It's going to absolutely ruin my business. I've been making very good money selling illegal videos to Zhuri. But the whole scheme depends on the government suppressing emotions. If they stop doing that, the videos I sell will become common as dirt, and the prices will collapse."

She lifted the fallen Zhuri up by his midsection and began to drag him back toward the door.

"What kind of videos were you selling?"

"Humorous ones. To trigger the laughter smell. Crude amateur stuff, mostly—household accidents, Zhuri falling down, flying into windows by mistake . . . the occasional Krik trying to eat something bigger than their head, then getting it stuck in their mouth . . ."

When she got back to the door with the unconscious Zhuri, she held his head up, placing his compound eye directly in front of the wall sensor.

The sensor beeped, and the door opened. Marf gently set the Zhuri down on the floor and began to help me step past him through the door.

"So . . . bloopers? You were selling blooper videos?"

"I don't know what that word means. But probably yes. When

I saw your *Birdleys* videos, I figured they'd be quite a hit. The Zhuri wouldn't understand the words, but they'd love the parts where the birds fly into things and get kicked in their reproductive organs."

We entered a large, high-ceilinged room that looked like a giant mausoleum. Hundreds of two-foot-by-two-foot square drawers filled three walls, stretching all the way to the ceiling. Along the near wall was a control panel. A pair of unconscious Zhuri lay slumped in front of it, along with a pair of prong weapons that they must have dropped when they fell.

Marf guided me to an empty stool next to the sleeping Zhuri. "Do me a favor and yell for your sister."

"Ila?" I yelled.

"Louder, please."

"ILA? ILAAAA? ARE YOU THERE?"

From somewhere up in the middle of the left-side wall came a muffled reply. *"Lan?"*

"Oh good," said Marf. "That's progress." She went to the control panel and began to press buttons on a screen as she kept talking. "So I sold a few of your *Birdleys* videos to my customers—"

"You promised you wouldn't do that!"

Marf shrugged. "It's not my fault you trusted me. I *did* tell you I was a criminal. Anyway, they went over even better than I'd expected. And if I'd just kept selling *The Birdleys,* I probably would've been fine. But then I made the mistake of showing one of your sister's music videos to a Zhuri customer. Personally, I don't care for that stuff. But Ezger had liked it, so I thought perhaps the Zhuri would too.

"And do you know what happened?" Marf turned her head to

look back at me. "The man absolutely lost his mind! Do you have any idea what a powerful effect music has on the Zhuri?"

I nodded. "I do now. I've seen it."

"I should've realized it was too hot to touch. But I got greedy. So I sold the ones I'd found on your sister's screen, and they spread like a virus. I barely had a chance to build her a guitar and record a new one before the government got wind of what was happening and came after me. The music was just too potent— they had to shut it down before the whole planet's emotions got out of control."

Marf looked up at the section of the wall where we'd heard Ila's voice. "I'm not quite sure how these holding cells operate— but I think this should do it." She pressed a button on the screen, and a two-by-two drawer in the middle of the wall twenty feet up began to open. I saw Ila's feet appear, followed by her legs.

The drawer began to tilt toward the floor. I gasped and stood up, but I was too woozy to run across the room. And even if I hadn't been, I couldn't have done anything to break her fall.

Fortunately, Marf could. She zipped over to the spot below Ila's drawer, getting there just in time to plop down on her back before Ila plummeted from above with a scream.

She bounced, feet first, off Marf's giant stomach.

"*MMRRMMFF!*" My translator beeped, I guess because it didn't recognize the Ororo word for "OOOOOOF!"

"Are you okay?"

Marf sat up. "I'll be sore tomorrow. But I'm fine now. Ila, how are you?"

Ila sat up, then nearly toppled over again. The neural disrupter was making her as dizzy as it made me. And without her translator, all she could do was stare, confused and scared, at Marf.

"Here!" I staggered over and handed Ila's earpiece and screen to her.

Marf stood up and waited for Ila to get her translator functioning. "I don't suppose you can walk any better than Lan?"

Ila got to her feet, took a step, and toppled into Marf.

"I'll take that as a no." Supporting Ila with one arm, Marf reached into her satchel with the other. She pulled out a small communicator and held it to her mouth.

"Ezger? I've got them both. Which exit should we take?"

Ezger's snappish growl came over the communicator, too faint for my translator to pick up.

"Oh dear," Marf replied. "That's not good at all. All right— we'll meet you in the back." She pocketed the communicator, then propped Ila against the nearest wall.

"What's not good?" I asked.

Marf headed toward the two unconscious Zhuri. "The electric fence around the prison just went down."

"Why is that bad?"

She bent down and picked up the two prong weapons from the floor. "I was counting on the fence to stand between us and a swarm of angry Zhuri. Here." She handed me one of the weapons. It was long and firm enough to support my weight like a walking stick. "You'll need this."

"To walk with? Or to fight with?"

"Both. Let's go."

23

THIS MIGHT GET MESSY

MARF HERDED ILA and me down a narrow series of twisting hallways as fast as we could go. Using the prong weapons as walking sticks, we were both able to walk without help, although we had a bad habit of crashing into the walls.

Marf was carrying two prong weapons of her own, plucked from some sleeping Zhuri we'd stepped over along the way. As we turned a corner, I tripped over another one, and he let out a squeak. Marf turned her head in alarm at the sound.

"They're starting to wake up. Move faster, please."

The whine of the protestors had gotten louder with every turn in the hallway. As we started down the last one, which dead-ended at a wide doorway, a new sound joined the whining— a flurry of rattling thuds that sounded like someone was pounding on a garbage can lid. As we approached the doorway, both the whining and the banging got so loud that Ila and I stopped, afraid to go any farther.

Marf squeezed past us. "Quickly!" She opened the door, and

the noise tripled in volume as she plunged into the unseen room. With no other choice, Ila and I followed.

It was a long garage, with four pods parked side by side. Each one faced a door wide enough for the pod to fly through. The room stank of Zhuri anger, and all four garage doors were shuddering under attacks from a shrieking swarm that was trying to break into the building from outside.

Marf was already halfway to the nearest pod. "QUICKLY! THANK YOU!"

As we staggered after her, I tried to ignore the rattling doors. The pod was locked, but Marf pulled some kind of gizmo from her satchel and used it to bypass the security system. The pod door opened, and she barged in, setting down her prong weapons as she headed to the control panel.

"Shut the pod door!" Ila and I got in and shut the door behind us.

"What can we do?" I asked.

"Sit down and hold on."

We did as we were told. I looked past Marf out the pod's front window. The garage door in front of us was shaking from the fury of the swarm on the other side.

The control panel's display lit up. Marf had managed to get the pod started with no password or key.

"Now all we need—" she started to say.

Just then, the garage door two pods down broke off its hinge, and a flying mob of shrieking Zhuri streamed inside.

"Oh dear." Marf pressed a button, and the garage door in front of our pod began to open, tilting outward on its upper hinge. The instant it did, the dozens of Zhuri who were rapidly filling up the garage realized where we were. Sprays of orange venom burst against the windows as they descended on us.

The garage door opened just wide enough to give us a glimpse of a seething mass of Zhuri on the other side, then shuddered to a stop as streaks of venom and flying Zhuri bodies blocked our view.

"Brace yourselves!" Marf yelled. The pod rose up and lurched forward. The swarming Zhuri in front of the pod scattered. I caught a glimpse of the half-open door ahead of us, and for a moment I thought we were going to bust through it and get free.

But the door was sturdier than it looked. When the pod struck it, there was a jarring crash, and all of our forward motion stopped. We skittered sideways, the pod's nose scraping along the door as heavy thuds landed on the ceiling and sides.

Dozens of Zhuri were hanging off the pod, trying to drag us down. And they were succeeding—even as the pod kept lurching sideways, I could feel us sinking.

Then the pod's nose lodged itself between the half-open door and the wall next to it. All the sideways movement stopped, and we dipped even farther. Marf kept throttling us forward, the whine from the stymied engine so loud that we could hear it over the screaming swarm.

The thudding got louder and more intense. Zhuri were hurling themselves at the pod's windows from all directions, trying to shatter them.

"Hold tight!" Marf yelled. Ila and I hung on to our seats as she changed course, and the pod lurched violently across the door.

"And again!" We lurched back in the opposite direction, so hard that I banged my head against the window.

"Backward!" There was a hard lurch backward, then a sudden, whiplashing stop as Marf put on the brakes just as we were about to hit the rear wall of the garage.

The pounding on the windows stopped, quickly replaced by a heavy orange spatter. Not wanting to be crushed by the unpredictable pod, the Zhuri were hanging back and spitting venom at us instead.

"Hold on!" Marf throttled the pod forward, taking another run at the door.

This time it broke open. We sailed forward, free of the building.

But we weren't free of the swarm. There were countless Zhuri in the air around the jail. As soon as we cleared the door, they began piling onto the sides and roof of the pod.

There must've been hundreds of them dragging us down, because even at full throttle, we moved like we were flying through thick mud. Once again, I could feel us sinking toward the ground.

"Ezger!" Marf yelled into her communicator. "Where *are* you?"

I heard Ezger bark a reply, but my translator couldn't catch it.

"I can't lift off!" Marf rumbled. "Find us and put up a fence! We'll run to you!"

With a bone-jarring jolt and a loud scraping noise, the pod hit the ground, its underpowered engine defeated by the weight of the swarm. Marf turned away from the control panel and picked up her two prongs. She flipped a switch on the side of each one, and blue electricity arced across their tips.

"Turn your weapons on!" I did as she said, praying I wasn't too dizzy to use it without accidentally zapping one of us instead of a Zhuri.

Their feet were hammering at the windows on all sides. It was only a matter of time before they shattered one.

Marf moved to the door, a prong in each hand. "Listen closely: Stand next to each other, just behind me. Put the prongs in your outer hands, pointed out. Keep your inner hands on my back. When I move, stay with me. Ezger's going to land my pod next to us, and we're going to run to it."

"They'll kill us!" Ila cried.

"They'll certainly try. I don't think they'll succeed. But it might get messy. Don't fall behind."

We stood, propping ourselves up with the fizzing prong weapons as we got into position behind the huge Ororo. I was on Ila's right, with my left hand on Marf's back and my right hand on my now-incredibly-dangerous walking stick.

I was still dizzy, and it felt like the whole pod was spinning. I wasn't sure if I could run even ten feet without toppling over, and the mass of Zhuri bodies hammering against the side of the pod was so thick that it seemed impossible for us to force our way through them.

"Are you sure this will work?" I yelled at Marf—but the last two words were swallowed by an electric thunderclap that lit everything up in a burst of blue light, blasting the swarm of Zhuri away from the pod door.

"NOW!"

Marf opened the door and barreled forward. Ila and I stumbled out behind her.

Marf's body was so big that I couldn't see anything ahead of us except the bright glow of an electric fence. The Zhuri screams coming from every direction were deafening. I tried to keep my eyes and my left hand on Marf's back while I leaned on the prong with my right, angling its business end away from Marf as I hobbled forward.

A stream of venom hit me from behind, drenching my right arm. I gripped the prong tighter as the pain shot through me. With my next step, I jabbed backward without looking and heard a *BZZZT!* that made me think I'd probably hit whoever had just spit on me.

Another scream came from right above me, and I looked up in time to see a Zhuri zooming in. I raised the prong, zapping him in the shoulder. The shock knocked him sideways, hard enough to bring down two other Zhuri along with him.

But raising the prong that high unbalanced me, and I'd lost my touch on Marf's back. I lowered the prong quickly, nearly hit myself in the face with it, and fell to my knees, almost dropping my weapon as I went down.

I looked ahead. Marf and Ila had both been hit with venom—there were streaks of orange running down their backs—but they were still moving forward.

And they were getting away from me.

I scrambled to my feet, staggered forward, and almost lost my balance again—but I managed to drive the butt of my weapon into the ground just in time to steady myself. As I took my next step, closing the distance between me and Marf, I got my first glimpse of what she was barreling toward.

Her silver pod was parked just ahead, a domed fence crackling in a ten-foot circle around it. The fence must've delivered some nasty shocks when it went up, because the ground just outside of it was littered with woozy, twitching Zhuri. There were only a handful of active ones within venom-spitting range of us, and Marf was using her prongs to zap them with both hands.

But beyond the narrow no-man's-land, the swarm had started to close in on us. And I had no idea how we were going to get past the fence that was protecting Marf's pod.

I caught up level with Ila, and my left hand found Marf's back just a few feet before she reached the buzzing fence. As I shifted my weight onto her big frame, it dawned on me that all three of us were about to be electrocuted.

The Zhuri realized it too. The whole swarm suddenly stopped and wheeled back as one, expecting an explosion of light and noise when Marf's enormous body met the high-voltage electricity.

But an instant before she touched the fence, it disappeared.

Marf barreled across its now-invisible line. As Ila and I followed her past it, screams of fury rose up from the swarm. They reversed course yet again, descending on us to resume their attack.

Then Ezger turned the fence back on.

There were earsplitting shrieks as a dozen Zhuri were zapped backward through the air. Ila and I both fell flat on our faces just inside the fence, safe from the swarm.

But not safe from the three Zhuri who'd managed to zoom inside the perimeter before the fence went back up.

Marf shocked two of them into twitchy helplessness.

The third one barfed venom all over my legs before I managed to zap it in the chest with my prong.

The pod door opened, and Ezger jumped out. He helped Ila and me inside as Marf clambered in and took over the controls. As soon as Ezger shut the door, the pod leaped into the sky.

A moment later, we'd left the swarm behind and were hurtling across the city at a few hundred miles an hour.

Marf's voice rumbled from the front of the pod. "Don't get venom on my carpet!"

"Too late," I groaned. The poisonous orange muck had soaked through my clothes, and the pain in my legs and arm was excruciating. My right arm and both legs were dripping wet, and the exposed skin on my hand was bright red and swelling up like an angry balloon. Next to me, Ila was grimacing in pain, her back and left side soaked with venom.

Fortunately, Marf had stocked the pod with antivenom cream. As we rocketed across the city, we wriggled out of our ruined clothes and frantically rubbed the medicine into our wounds.

It fixed the pain and swelling. But there was nothing we could do for my blue cotton shirt and navy pants, or Ila's peasant blouse and faded jeans.

"Do you absolutely *have* to wear clothes?" Marf asked.

Ila and I looked at each other in our ragged underwear. "We'd definitely prefer it."

Marf sighed. "It's a silly custom. But fine." She fetched some kind of portable 3-D printer from a storage space in the back of the pod. A minute later, Ila and I were putting on makeshift overalls that looked—and, worse, felt—like they were made from plastic garbage bags.

But the garbage-bag clothes were the least of our worries.

We had a government to overthrow.

24

A PERFECT PLAN, EXCEPT FOR THAT ONE HORRIBLE PART

ILA WAS FLABBERGASTED. "We're going to *what*?"

"Overthrow the government," Marf told her. "At this point, I'm afraid it's your only alternative to certain death."

"But how?"

"That depends on how things are playing out on Zhuri television."

As she trundled past me to a TV screen on the pod's back wall, the landscape outside the window—which had been zipping by so fast that it was a blur—rapidly changed from the usual beige to a reddish-orange color I'd never seen before.

Then, in a split second, the pod came to a dead stop in midair.

"How does it *do* that?" I asked.

"Do what?"

"Stop and start so fast without us feeling anything. We should've gone through the front windshield just now."

"It would take several days to explain the technology," said Marf as she turned on the TV.

"Where *are* we?" Ila was staring out the window next to me.

The pod had descended to land on the floor of what looked like a narrow desert canyon. Giant rocks were scattered across it, casting gloomy shadows in the fading light just before sunset.

"It's the empty quarter beyond the city," said Ezger. "The government won't think to search for us here."

Marf gestured toward the TV screen. "Look—we're on television."

The Zhuri news channel was broadcasting drone-camera footage of our escape. When I saw the size of the swarm surrounding the prison, I gasped. While we'd been fighting our way through it, I hadn't been able to see more than a few yards in any direction. But what I'd witnessed of the swarm turned out to have been just a tiny piece of the total. There must've been a hundred thousand Zhuri mobbing the building.

". . . dozens of citizens injured in their escape. The human animals and their accomplices, pictured here—"

The image switched to a screen split four ways. On the top were grainy still photos of Ila and me, taken from drone cameras when we were entering school. On the bottom were what looked like mug shots of Marf and Ezger.

"—are violent and dangerous . . ."

"I do wish they wouldn't use our school photos," Marf rumbled.

"I don't mind," said Ezger. "I look very handsome in mine."

"Shhh!" The broadcast had switched to a Zhuri government official making an announcement:

". . . all restrictions on the use of venom are suspended. Everyone agrees the human animals are a threat that must be destroyed."

"This is amazing news!" Marf exclaimed.

I was shocked. "They're telling people to *kill* us!"

"Don't worry about that. Ezger's right—they'll never find us here. And this news is truly amazing!"

"How is telling people to kill us 'amazing'?"

The newscast switched to a shot of a massive swarm. At first I thought it was the one from the prison.

"The other two humans are currently being held . . ."

"Because it means—" Marf began to explain.

"Shhhhh!" hissed Ila. "It's our parents!"

The swarm was so big that it was hard to tell what the Zhuri were swarming. All I could see beneath the horde was the pulsing blue glow of an electric fence under attack.

". . . spaceport to depart from the planet. But the human animals are causing such strong emotion among the Zhuri public that all traffic in and out of the spaceport has been halted . . ."

"They're attacking Mom and Dad!" Ila cried.

We all stared closely at the swarm and the fence lighting up beneath it. "That's definitely the spaceport," Ezger said. "They're probably being kept in a hangar under that fence. Immigration must be protecting them, or the fence would've come down already."

"We've got to do something!" I yelled.

"But that's the amazing part," said Marf. "The government's about to collapse on its own! We just have to wait it out."

"How do you figure?"

She pointed at the screen with a big, stubby finger. "Look at what's missing from this scene: soldiers. There weren't any outside your prison either."

"So?"

"So the government's abandoned the one job they were put in power to do. The whole reason the traditionalists took over from the progressives was to *prevent swarms from ever forming.* That's why they tried to eliminate emotions in the first place. And on the rare occasions in the past twenty years when a swarm's started to form, they've always sent soldiers to zap everyone back into line.

"But they're not even *trying* to stop these swarms. The government's encouraging them! They're so scared of the emotions you humans might stir up, and so desperate to get rid of you, that they're practically *begging* the swarms to destroy you! It's the exact opposite of what people expect from their leadership. And once everyone's calmed down in a day or two, the whole planet will be so ashamed of itself for what the government's allowing to happen that they'll replace it with new leaders from the other faction. Just like they did after the Nug massacre."

As I realized what that meant, my whole body started to shake with fear. "But they'll kill our parents!"

Marf's eyes scrunched up in a pained look. "That *is* the one downside. And I'm terribly sorry—"

"WE'VE GOT TO STOP THEM!" screamed Ila. She pointed to the control panel. "Fly us to the spaceport!"

"That'd be madness," Marf replied. "Look at the size of that swarm! And it's only going to get larger—you think all those Zhuri who were swarming the prison are just calling it a day and heading home? By the time we get to the spaceport, it'll be twice the size. Your parents will likely be dead already. Then the swarm will turn on us."

"I don't care! I'm flying us there!" Ila yelled, running for the controls.

"Good luck starting the engine," Ezger told her.

"There's got to be something we can do!" I told Marf.

"There is," she said. "We wait here. Within a day or two, the government will collapse, and a new one will form. They'll let your whole ship full of humans land! It's what you've wanted all along."

"WE CAN'T LET MY PARENTS DIE!"

"I know it sounds awful—"

"FLY THIS THING!" Ila screamed at Marf, pounding the control panel in frustration.

"To where?" Marf asked her. "Certain death? If we went to the spaceport, what good could we possibly do?"

I stared at the swarm on the TV. It was pulsing with rage—there were so many of them, all lunging in unison at the fence, that they looked less like a hundred thousand Zhuri than a single giant, seething animal.

It was the nightmare version of the dreamy, shimmering crowd that had danced to Ila's music in the lunchroom.

What if . . . ?

"What if we turn the swarm?" I asked.

All three of them turned to stare at me. "Music's incredibly powerful to them. Right? That's why the government's so scared of it. So if we went there and played music for the swarm—something calm and soothing—maybe we could stop it. Turn that anger into something positive. It's possible, right?"

Marf didn't say anything.

"Right?" I repeated.

Marf let out a deep, rumbling sigh. "Maybe. It's hard to know. No one's ever tried anything like that. And do you have any idea how dangerous it would be? To play music loud enough to be heard over the sound of that swarm, we'd have to fly in very close. And the spaceport's not like the prison—it has defenses to protect it from air attack. If we show up and start buzzing around in the sky, they'll try to shoot us down with pulse weapons."

" 'Try'? Or 'will'? Can't your fancy pod protect us?"

"Maybe. I can't be sure. I'm not even sure if it's possible to turn the swarm. But if we just stay here, eventually the government will fall—"

"And our parents will die!" Ila screamed.

"And if we go to the spaceport, we'll die with them!" I'd never heard Marf's voice reach such a high pitch. "It's *very* risky!"

"No offense to you humans," said Ezger, "but you're really being stupid about this."

"What if it was *your* parents?" I asked him.

He shrugged. "Krik aren't sentimental like that. My parents would be mad at me if I *did* try to save them."

I turned to Marf. "What about yours?"

She sighed again, so heavily that her whole body rippled. Then she crossed over to a storage cabinet.

"COME ON!" Ila screamed.

"Stop yelling at me," Marf scolded her. "It's not helping."

She opened the cabinet and pulled out the same red-and-gold guitar that the government soldiers had taken from our house. She headed back to the control panel, holding the guitar out for Ila.

"Hurry up and tune this," Marf said. "Once we take off, we'll be over the spaceport in a few minutes."

Ila's eyes lit up. "How did you get it back from the government?"

"I didn't. I made two of them and kept this one." She looked at Ezger. "Are you coming with us? Or do you want to get out of the pod now?"

Ezger looked out the window at the scattered boulders on the canyon floor. "You mean, would I rather go sit alone on that rock . . . or fly into a swarm of a quarter million screaming Zhuri armed with pulse weapons and just sort of *hope* the little human music machine magically turns them peaceful?"

"You don't have to be so negative," Marf told him.

Ezger opened the pod door. "Best of luck. You're all out of your minds."

As we flew away, I had to admit Ezger looked very comfortable sitting alone on his rock.

25

CAN SWEET SOUNDS SOOTHE A SAVAGE SWARM?

ILA WAS SITTING in the back of the pod, tuning the guitar as a tiny microphone drone hovered in front of her. I was up front with Marf, looking out over the darkening city as we rocketed across it in the twilight.

"The microphone's not working!" Ila yelled.

"I haven't turned it on!" Marf yelled back at her. "Don't worry—the external speakers are quite powerful. When the time comes, they'll be able to hear you."

Then she turned to me and lowered her voice. "The hardest part in all this will be dodging those pulse weapons. They're likely to start firing as soon as they realize who we are."

"And if one hits us, we'll blow up?"

"Not instantly. The pulse will just disable the engine. The blowing-up part will happen when we hit the ground."

"So how do we avoid that?"

"By not staying in one place long enough for the weapons to target us. Once we're over the swarm, I'll program the pod to change its location a few times a second. That should keep us safe from the pulses. Unfortunately, it also means we'll have to black out the windows."

"Why?"

"Because human and Ororo brains can't process such quick changes in their visual environment. Thanks to the ship's inertial buffer, we won't feel anything. But if we looked out the window, we'd get so disoriented that we'd vomit all over ourselves."

"If we can't look out the window, how are we going to know if the music's working?"

"We'll keep the TV on and hope they keep broadcasting live."

I checked the screen above and behind Ila. The news was showing a live feed of the swarm at the spaceport. Just like Marf had predicted, it was getting larger by the second as a steady stream of Zhuri joined it, probably from the group that had attacked us at the prison.

Marf raised her voice, calling out to Ila. "Twenty seconds! Are you ready?"

She strummed the guitar. "I hope so."

I went back to sit across from Ila. "Anything I can do for you?"

Blackout shades came down over all the windows, shutting us off from the outside world. Ila looked alarmed—she hadn't heard Marf's explanation. "Why is that happening?"

"Ten seconds!" Marf called out.

"It's too long a story," I told Ila. "Don't worry about it."

Marf cut off the sound on the TV—and, for the first time, I heard the noise of the approaching swarm. As we zoomed in and the screams rose in volume, I looked back up at the TV. There were so many Zhuri clustered together now that I could barely see the glow from the fence they were attacking.

"Five . . . four . . . ," Marf called out.

The glow from the fence flickered, growing much brighter for an instant. Then it vanished.

The swarm had broken through the fence protecting Mom and Dad. I gasped, but the sound was drowned out by the rising noise of the crowd.

"Three . . . two . . ."

Ila saw the look on my face and turned around to see what I was staring at. The swarm was collapsing inward as the Zhuri at the bottom of it rushed into the empty space to attack the hangar where our parents were being held.

". . . one . . ." I could barely hear Marf's voice over the shrieks of the swarm.

"OHMYGOSH!"

"Don't look!" I yelled at Ila. "Just play!"

"Microphone on!"

A green indicator lit up on the drone mic as the stink of Zhuri anger began to fill the pod. We were right on top of the swarm now.

Ila stared at me, her eyes wide with fear. The shrieks of the swarm were deafening. Hoping Marf's speakers were loud enough to cut through the racket, I pantomimed strumming the guitar.

Ila didn't move. She just kept staring at me in horror. I pantomimed strumming again.

C'mon, Ila! Play!

She squeezed her eyes shut and swept her hand down on the opening chord of "Under a Blue Sky."

The speakers were every bit as loud as Marf had promised. The sound was so huge that it made my ears ring.

Ila flinched at the volume but kept playing.

I looked up at the screen. Our pod blinked into view, a tiny drop above the ocean of angry Zhuri. It showed up so fast that it seemed to have come out of nowhere.

Then, just as quickly, it disappeared . . . only to reappear again, above and to the left of where I'd first seen it.

It vanished again . . . reappeared . . . vanished again . . .

In less than two seconds, the pod changed positions half a dozen times, moving in random directions at speeds so fast that the Zhuri TV camera couldn't even record the movement.

It was obvious why Marf had to black out the windows. Thanks to the inertial buffer, I didn't feel any of the changes in speed and direction. But just watching the pod zip around on TV made me woozy. Looking out the windows, even from the corner of my eye, would've been unbearable.

As Ila's amplified chords crashed like waves in my ears, I tried to ignore the pod zipping around and watch the swarm's reaction instead. It seemed to contract on every downbeat, lunging farther down toward the hangar. On the upbeat, it expanded again.

A burst of white light appeared in the sky above the swarm, winking on and off like a strobe. Another one followed it, in a different part of the sky. Then there were three at once, going off in a cluster like flashbulbs, so bright that they left spots in my eyes.

They were firing at us.

Within a few seconds, so many pulses were flashing on the TV screen that I couldn't have located our pod in the middle of them if I'd tried. All I could see were the swarm and the bursts of pulse weapons above it.

Ila reached the end of the "Blue Sky" guitar intro, opened her mouth, and began to sing.

> *Well, the nights have been black*
> *And the days have been gray*

A shiver went down my spine. It had been ages since I'd heard my sister sing live, and I'd forgotten how powerful her voice was, especially when it was being amplified to a hundred times its normal volume.

When Ila's vocals reached the swarm, it shuddered like it had been hit with a hammer. On the third line of the vocal, it started to sway.

Until the singing started, the swarm's energy had been mostly up and down, pressing its attack on the hangar below. But as more and more Zhuri began to fall under the spell of Ila's voice, its energy shifted sideways. Slowly but surely, the swarm began to move in the same left-right-left shimmy that I'd seen in the cafeteria.

The smell of gasoline still filled the pod, but honeysuckle and mint were starting to compete with it.

When Ila got to the chorus, she changed a single word:

> *I want to live under a green sky*
> *Don't want to numb the pain just to get by*

As it swayed, the swarm began to expand upward. The Zhuri were gradually shifting their attention from the hangar below them to the music that was pouring out of the speakers from above.

It's working! She's turning the swarm!

Ila leaned over her guitar, eyes closed, blind to everything except the song she was singing. The drone mic hovered in the air at chest level, halfway between her mouth and the guitar's sound hole.

I looked back at Marf. She was fussing over the control panel. When I turned again to look at the TV behind Ila, the swarm had expanded up to fill most of the empty sky where the pulse weapon's bursts had been winking on and off.

Then the image disappeared, replaced by a Zhuri newscaster in some kind of TV studio. Whoever was in charge of the broadcast had stopped showing the swarm live.

They'd been trying to prove to the whole planet just how violent and terrible emotions were. But what was happening now wasn't terrible at all.

It was beautiful.

So they'd shut off the cameras.

We were winning.

Ila was on her third verse. I couldn't see the swarm anymore, but I could smell it—and while the gasoline was still strong, the honeysuckle and mint were slowly starting to overpower it.

As she went into the bridge after the third chorus of the song, Ila opened her eyes for the first time. She saw the grin on my face and relayed it back to me with a smile of her own.

Then the pulse weapon hit us.

It must've knocked out the inertial buffer, because suddenly I was upside down on the far side of the pod, with a searing pain in my side from having been thrown against the back of a chair at high speed.

Then a second pulse hit us, and we fell from the sky.

26

DYING ONSTAGE

BZZZZZT!

BZZZZZT!

I was lying in a heap on the floor of the pod, squashed against the base of a chair. Somewhere, a fence was buzzing.

The windows were still blacked out. An emergency light was on, giving the whole compartment a sickly green color.

The swarm had turned again. Outside, they were screaming.

Inside, it stank of gasoline.

I got up onto my knees. Everything hurt.

There was blood. Not all of it seemed to be mine.

Ila's legs were sticking out from behind a chair. I crawled over to her.

"Ila? Ila!"

She raised her head to reveal an ugly, still-bleeding gash that ran across her temple into her hairline. Her eyes opened just wide enough to look at me.

"Muggh." She shut her eyes and slumped back down again.

BZZZZZZT! BZZZZZZT!

The screams were getting louder, and the buzzing was getting more frequent. The swarm was stepping up its attack.

"*Ila?* Can you still sing?"

Her eyes fluttered.

"Ila!"

"Nuugh."

"Get up! Please?"

She wouldn't answer. But at least she was alive.

BZZZZZT!

BZZZZZT!

BZZZZZT!

I staggered to my feet. Marf was in the front of the pod, her body drooped over the control panel. As I made my way over to her, I almost tripped over the guitar. It was broken in half, the neck hanging by the strings from its cracked body.

"Marf!"

Her eyes opened. *"MRRRRMMMM."*

I waited for the translation in my ear, but it didn't come. My earpiece was gone, lost somewhere in the wreck of the pod.

BZZZZZT! BZZZZZT! BZZZZZT!

Marf must've turned on the fence before we crashed. Either that or the pod had deployed it automatically.

But soon enough, the swarm would bust through.

Somebody had to do something.

I was the only one standing.

I lurched to the door and opened it.

At first all I could see was the crackling blue light of the fence, surrounding me in every direction. I blinked it away, and when my eyes adjusted, the sight of thousands of frenzied

Zhuri—all shrieking at me from just beyond the fence's ten-foot perimeter—made my knees buckle.

A moment ago, Ila's music had put them on a knife's edge between angry and happy.

But when the music had stopped, they'd tipped back into anger.

Now they wanted to kill me. The thought of it was making them scream even louder.

BZZZZZZT! A Zhuri threw his body against the fence.

BZZZZZZT! BZZZZZZT! Two more.

BZZZZZZT! BZZZZZZT! BZZZZZZT!

What can I do?

I couldn't sing. I was terrible at it.

Even if I could, they wouldn't have been able to hear me. It was too loud.

Where's that drone mic?

It didn't matter. What was I going to say that could stop a swarm?

Hey, there! I just flew in from Earth, and boy, are my arms tired!

Actually . . .

Maybe . . .

It'll never work.

But I've got to try it anyway.

I raised my leg as high as I could, bringing it down in a long, bendy-legged stride. Then I did the same with the other leg, slowly walking forward in the most exaggerated, silly-looking Zhuri impression I could manage.

The Zhuri closest to the fence drew their heads back in surprise.

The other quarter of a million didn't notice. Most of them couldn't even see me. They were just feeding off each other's anger.

I kept going, bobbing up and down like a jack-in-the-box, until I was only a step away from the fence. I took as long a stride as I dared—getting so close to the electrical field that my hair stood up—then sprang backward off my lead foot, pretending to get zapped by the fence.

I landed hard on my butt, expecting to get a bounce from the usual spongy floor.

But we were outside, on the hard tarmac of the spaceport. I didn't get any bounce at all. Instead I almost broke my tailbone.

Ouch . . .

Hopefully, that made it funnier.

I staggered to my feet. The shrieks of the Zhuri filled my ears. I couldn't smell anything except gasoline.

But the fence hadn't buzzed since I'd started my slapstick routine. That was progress.

I did it again, bounce-walking up to the fence, then pratfalling backward like I'd been zapped. The landing hurt even worse the second time.

As I got up, I heard a rumble behind me.

"MRRRRMMMM!"

Marf was standing in the open door of the pod. When our eyes met, she winked.

I was trying to figure out what the wink meant when there was a piercing scream and the fence lit up. I turned just in time to catch a glimpse of a Zhuri bouncing off of it, knocking several others out of the air like bowling pins.

Not everybody was enjoying the comedy.

"MRRRRRM!"

I turned back to Marf. She was waddling toward me—much more slowly and clumsily than I knew she was capable of moving—with her hands raised, like she wanted to strangle me.

I was so confused that I stood frozen in place until her giant paws were almost around my neck. At the last second, I came to my senses and ducked out of the way, diving under her outstretched hands.

I tumbled to the ground. When I got myself turned around, Marf was already headed back my way. Her hands were outstretched again, and her waddle was so pronounced that the flesh was sloshing back and forth on her frame like water in a stirred-up bathtub.

It's like she's trying *to look ridiculous.*

Ooooooh. Right . . .

I limped to my feet and ran away from her in an exaggerated, bendy-legged Zhuri imitation. As she chased me in a circle around the pod—moving just fast enough that I stayed an arm's length out of reach—the Zhuri closest to the fence began to draw back again, their tubelike mouths going limp.

But they were the only ones in the swarm who could see us. Even as they drew back, the crowd behind them kept pushing forward in anger. Every couple of seconds, someone from the middle of the swarm pushed his way through to the front, screaming in fury as he flung his body against the fence. When it zapped him back, it knocked out a big chunk of the front row, and the screamers behind them would rush into the breach.

We were losing fans as fast as we were making them.

Marf and I made three full circles of the fence, stopping at every turn for a fake grappling session. By the end of it, I was panting and sweaty.

But the screams of anger were as loud as they'd ever been.

At the end of a long loop, I stopped and turned, planting myself a couple of feet in front of the fence. Marf lumbered at me, her hands raised.

I ducked under her arms again, tumbling past her to land on my stomach.

But I'd planted myself too close to the fence. Marf couldn't stop in time. She hit the wall of electrical current with an earsplitting *BZZZZZZT!* and toppled backward, collapsing on top of me.

I was buried alive under six hundred pounds of unconscious Ororo.

"MRRRF!"

I could barely hear my own yell. The screams of the swarm and the buzzing of the fence were muffled like I was underwater. I tried to kick and squirm, but there was just too much Marf on top of me.

I couldn't move. I couldn't breathe. I was going to suffocate.

The muffled screams were getting louder. The buzzing was almost nonstop now.

My cheek was pressed against the pavement. I tried to suck in air, but there wasn't any.

Fireworks appeared in my eyes. I was blacking out from lack of oxygen.

At least it beats death by venom. . . .

Then I was gone.

Dead.

I could hear an angel in the distance, welcoming me to heaven with her song:

Mid pleasures and palaces though we may roam
Be it ever so humble, there's no place like home
A charm from the skies seems to hallow us there
Which through the world is never met elsewhere

Such a pretty song, I thought to myself. *My sister used to sing it.*
That angel sounds just like my sister did.
Maybe death isn't so bad.

Ila's singing must've woken up Marf. She rolled off me with a rumbling groan. As I coughed and sputtered for breath, Ila's second verse filled my ears.

Home! Home!
Sweet, sweet home
There's no place like home
There's no place like home

She was standing at the pod door, eyes squeezed shut, blood still trickling down the side of her face from the gash in her head as she belted the song into the drone mic.

It was a good thing her eyes were shut. If they'd been open, she might have fainted at the sight of a quarter million Zhuri starting to sway as one over her head.

After she finished "Home, Sweet Home," she broke into "What a Wonderful World."

She followed that with "Tomorrow."

243

She'd just launched into "Over the Rainbow" when the swarm parted in front of us. A group of Zhuri led Mom and Dad through the crowd to the edge of the fence. They had to wait for a minute while Marf—still half-wrecked from the fence's neural disrupter—dragged herself back to the pod's control panel and shut the fence off.

Everybody hugged and cried, and the first thing Dad asked was why we were wearing garbage bags. We started to explain, but the swarm was getting restless over our heads, and we figured Ila should start singing again ASAP.

So my sister dried her tears, and after Mom bound up the gash on her head with fabric that Dad tore from the bottom of his shirt, Ila went back to belting out songs.

She didn't stop until her voice gave out two hours later.

But the fence never went back up, because we didn't need it anymore.

If there was an announcement on the news that the government had changed hands, we missed it. By the time we dug our earpieces out of the wreckage of Marf's pod, they were already reporting that "everyone agreed" the humans and their music were welcome to stay on Planet Choom.

27

PROGRAMMING TRANSCRIPT
CHOOM TELEVISION CHANNEL FIVE
DAY 162 AHA (AFTER HUMAN ARRIVAL)

LAN: Welcome back to the Human Channel's afternoon comedy block! I'm your host, Lan Mifune!

NAYA: And I'm Naya Hadid! You're watching the *Ed and Fred* season four marathon, and that was episode six, "Fred Gets a Puppy!"

LAN: With us in the studio today, our usual panel of interspecies comedy fans: Marf, Ezger, and Iruu. So! What did everybody think of this one?

IRUU: It was very funny! Especially when the new puppy left his body garbage all over the house. But it was also sad and upsetting. I did not understand why Fred made the puppy his prisoner.

LAN: That's not actually what happened—

MARF: Of course it is. Fred attached a collar to the puppy's neck and dragged it places against its will. And at night he locked it in a crate. How was it not his prisoner?

NAYA: It wasn't like that on Earth! We loved our pets. And they loved us!

MARF: You are fooling yourselves. They could not possibly have loved you. You were oppressing them.

IRUU: Perhaps they only pretended to love you in exchange for food? That would make more sense.

EZGER: There was not nearly enough food in this episode.

MARF: You say that about every episode.

EZGER: It is always true. Except for that episode about the eating holiday.

LAN: You mean, the Thanksgiving episode?

EZGER: Yes. Although I hated that one too. They should have eaten the bird *before* it was dead.

NAYA: I feel like we've had this argument before. . . .

EZGER: Many times. And you are always wrong about it.

LAN: As much as I'd love to rehash the food argument, it's time to read the news. Whole lot of stuff happening in the human community today. Right, Naya?

NAYA: There sure is! And it all starts on the suswut field. Last night was the season opener for Choom's Regional League Three—and for the first time in planetary history, a team of humans competed! Head coach Dave Gunderson's Fightin' Ninety-Niners squared off against Team Seven Eight! And lost by a score of . . . oh, wow: thirty-three thousand six hundred and twelve . . . to zero.

LAN: Is that even possible?

IRUU: It is. I watched this game on television. It was very sad. Everyone agrees humans are not good at suswut.

EZGER: And yet suswut is so critically important to all our lives. It is definitely not a pointless and stupid game that serves no purpose.

IRUU: I agree it is not that! And I am pleasantly surprised you feel this way, Ezger.

MARF: He doesn't. Do you remember last week's panel discussion? When we explained what "sarcasm" means?

IRUU: Oh! I do remember that. Ezger, were you using sarcasm just now?

EZGER: Of course not. I would never use sarcasm. Especially not when talking about suswut. Watching groups of Zhuri fly through the air and throw things at each other is certainly *not* a complete waste of everyone's time.

NAYA: Ooookay . . . back to the news!

LAN: Yes! Moving on to the world of education: open enrollment begins today for the Iseeyii Interspecies Academy's adult extension courses in music, animation, and improv comedy. All skill levels and species are welcome, so whether you're human, Zhuri, Krik, or Ororo, if you want to get involved in the cultural life of our planet and have *tons of fun* while you're at it, come on down!

NAYA: This is so important, people. Especially the animation classes! We are desperate for new animation talent!

LAN: We really are. Can't keep playing *Birdleys* reruns forever, folks! Gotta start making some new stuff! Give a little back to this planet that's been so good to all of us! What other news have you got, Naya?

NAYA: Couple of *very* big stories in music today. First up, the joint Ororo-Human Task Force on Musical Technology just announced a major breakthrough: engineers working from data collected in human video archives believe they have successfully manufactured an oboe!

LAN: Oh, that *is* big. Marf, aren't you on that task force?

MARF: I am. And I must say, reconstructing the oboe was an even bigger challenge than the trombone. But I should point out that this breakthrough has not been confirmed yet. We won't know if the oboe was a success until someone actually learns how to play it.

LAN: Fingers crossed—and if any of you watching at home think you've got what it takes to make actual music come out of what we're almost but not quite sure is a working oboe, please contact the Task Force on Musical Technology ASAP!

NAYA: Last but not least—the biggest music news in months! Do you want to handle this one, Lan? It's pretty close to home.

LAN: Yes! The new Ila Mifune album is finally complete!

IRUU: Oh, that is wonderful!

EZGER: I agree! And I am not even being sarcastic.

LAN: It'll be available for planetwide download on Human Music Frequency One starting tonight! And to mark the release, Ila's going to play a free concert tomorrow evening at the Nug Memorial Concert Grounds outside the city.

IRUU: I cannot wait for this concert! Everyone agrees Ila Mifune is the biggest star on the planet!

MARF: Not if you're an Ororo. We find human voices squeaky and irritating. We'll be staying home and watching TV that night.

NAYA: If you do, keep it on the Human Channel—we've got you covered with a *Birdleys* season ten marathon start-